The Rink Girl

Stories

The Rink Girl

Stories by Mark Brazaitis

Hollywood Books International

Published by
Hollywood Books International
the fiction imprint of Press Americana
americanpopularculture.com

This book is a work of fiction, a product of the author's imagination. Any relation to actual character, place, incident, or any other matter is purely coincidental.

Cover Art: Ian Hylands
Cover Design: Lisa Bridges

Library of Congress Cataloging-in-Publication Data

Names: Brazaitis, Mark, 1966- author.
Title: The rink girl : stories / by Mark Brazaitis.
Description: [Hollywood, California] : Hollywood Books International, 2018.
Identifiers: LCCN 2018023288 | ISBN 9780996777988 (softcover)
Classification: LCC PS3552.R3566 A6 2018 | DDC 813/.54--dc23
LC record available at https://lccn.loc.gov/2018023288

I am deeply grateful to my wife, Julie, and my daughters, Annabel and Rebecca. A triple-axel thank-you to Rebecca's coaches present and past: Angela Barclay, Gina Geils, Shaun Adams Butler, Courtney Ann Caldwell, Alicia Marcucci, and Paul Wylie. They are all marvelous.

TABLE OF CONTENTS

DEAR KRISTI YAMAGUCHI

October 1, 1991

Dear Kristi,

I am writing to you because I love how you skate. I know you will win the gold medal at the Olympics.

Some people think I'm an amazing skater. Mom still calls me Alice Marvelous even though she hasn't seen me skate in two months. She's too tired.

Mom doesn't drive me to the rink anymore, so I walked again today. It isn't far. Two miles. Ivan, my coach, tells me I should think of the walk as off-ice training. "Good for thighs," he says. He's Russian. He lives here because his wife is studying biology at the university (Ohio Eastern). He was a Russian national champion in pairs skating.

By the way, I'm thirteen years old. I'm in the eighth grade at Sherman Middle School. I have two of your posters.

Sincerely,

Alice Maravicious

P.S. I don't know how I will mail you this letter. I don't have your address.

October 3, 1991

Dear Kristi,

Today at the rink, Bev was talking to Gisela, the French exchange student, about God. Bev is a junior in high school. She calls herself a "melting pot in one person" because her father is from Sweden and her mother is from Antigua and her grandfather was one of the leaders of the Carnation Revolution in Portugal. (She said he used flowers instead of guns, but she was joking. I think.) Sometimes Bev wears her long, black hair in a ponytail. Sometimes she doesn't, and it dances around her face, which is the color of "a sunrise dipped in coffee" (her words). Bev told Gisela that God is never in church because God would never want to be so bored. God, she said, is in places where there is elation.

Gisela asked Bev what elation means, but I knew because I like to read. When I need a break from skating, I sit by the fire in the lobby and read books I find in Dad's study. (He's an English professor.) I am reading a book called *Anna Karenina*, which is about a sad woman who doesn't like her husband.

Gisela asked Bev where there is elation. Bev said, "Right here." She spread her arms wide like Jesus. Gisela thought she was joking (so did I), but Bev flew around the rink, shouting like a preacher, "This is the house of the holy!"

My family is Catholic, but we don't go to church anymore. Mom is too tired to go anywhere except, sometimes, to the doctor.

Sincerely,

Alice

October 4, 1991

Dear Kristi,

Gisela doesn't do doubles yet, but Ivan says she skates "like angel." He winked at me and said, "And you skate like devil."

Is it better to skate like an angel or like the devil?

Sincerely,

Alice "the Devil" Maravicious

October 6, 1991

Dear Kristi,

Danny, my younger brother (nine years old), asked me this morning if Mom has cancer.

I told him she didn't.

"Why is she in bed all the time?" he asked.

"Because she works hard," I said.

"But when does she work?" he said. "She doesn't have a job."

"She works hard on her paintings."

"I don't ever see her painting."

"She looks after you and me," I said.

"But after school, I'm at Kaleidoscope and you're at the rink."

"There is a lot you don't know about adults," I said. "Believe me, okay?"

I think he believed me. But I didn't believe myself. Does Mom have cancer?

Your concerned friend,

Alice

October 7, 1991

Dear Kristi,

Mom doesn't have cancer! I asked her and she said, no, 100 percent no.

I was super, super relieved and super, super happy.

But now I'm worried she has something else.

Your fellow skater,

Alice

October 9, 1991

Dear Kristi,

Today, Mr. Williams, the rink manager, let me stay past the end of the freestyle session to practice my double axel. When I came off the ice after landing it three times in a row, Bev was in the lobby. She had come back to the rink because she'd left her math book in the locker room. "I'm not surprised you're still here," she said to me. "You work harder than any skater I know."

She said she and her mom wanted to give me a ride home. "It's dark," Bev said. "And the police haven't caught the Sherman Strangler."

The Sherman Strangler is what the newspaper (*Sherman Advocate and Post*) calls the man who killed two women in the trailer park behind Sherman Elementary School. He killed one of the women last week and one of the women three weeks ago.

I guess I should be scared of the Sherman Strangler. So I said yes to a ride.

In the car, Bev's mom, who looks like Bev except with darker skin, said because of the Sherman Strangler she checks three times a night to make sure all her doors are locked.

I said, "My dad bought a gun."

He bought it because the Sherman Strangler, he said, "is not going to strangle us." He said he was going to put the gun in a special place known only to him and Mom.

Bev's mom said, "I don't like guns, but I understand."

I said, "My mom doesn't like guns either. She's a pacifist." I remembered this word because it's like pacifier. I remember when Danny sucked on a pacifier. Sometimes I wish I could stick a pacifier in his mouth now, especially when he's asking Mom and Dad if he can have a dog.

I might like a dog, but Danny is too young to take care of it, Dad is never home, Mom is in bed all the time, and I spend three-quarters of my life at the rink.

If dogs could skate, I might change my mind.

Do you have a dog?

Sincerely,

Alice

PS I stopped reading *Anna Karenina*. It is too long and too sad. And too boring.

October 11, 1991

Dear Kristi,

Last night, I heard Mom tell Dad she was tired of him treating his classes like *The Love Connection*. I was supposed to be asleep, but sometimes I can't sleep, especially when the moon is full. Or half full. Or grinning at me like a cat.

Mom said, "Tell me she's at least a sophomore this time."

He laughed the way he does when he thinks she's being crazy.

Is Mom crazy? She cries a lot, over weird stuff. Like when she found Danny's old blue blanket in a drawer. Like when she found a portrait she painted of me when I was six. In the portrait, I'm wearing a gold medal.

I remember how Mom used to paint and sing and help me with my homework and clean Danny's room and make dinner—all at the same time!

I remember Dad saying that even if you added up me and him and Danny, we didn't have half the energy Mom did.

I remember how when I played Alice in "Alice in Wonderland on Ice" last year, she came to all three shows and applauded the loudest and longest of anyone. (I was embarrassed.)

Where did she go?

Sincerely,

Alice

October 14, 1991

Dear Kristi,

Today as I was walking back from the rink, I saw Dad's car coming from the other direction. I knew it was Dad driving because he wasn't looking at the road. He was looking at the person sitting next to him, which he always does when he tells stories. At first, I thought she was Mom. She had the same black hair and pale skin. But she was smiling, so I knew she wasn't Mom.

Dad never saw me.

Sincerely,

Alice

P.S. Bev said if I mail these letters to the U.S. Figure Skating Association, someone will give them to you.

October 16, 1991

Dear Kristi,

I asked Danny today what kind of dog he wants, and he said, "A gold dog."

I said, "Do you mean a golden retriever or a golden lab?"

He said, "I don't care. If it's gold, it will make Mom happy."

I said I didn't see how.

"A gold dog is like sunshine," he said. "Sunshine makes people happy."

I said it might be easier if she just walked outside.

Do you have a brother?

Sincerely,

Alice

October 17, 1991

Dear Kristi,

Ivan was late for my lesson, so for an hour today I had the rink all to myself. I made up a program to "Song of Me," which is by a singer named Becca Bishop. She used to live in Sherman. Here are the words I like:

The best company I find
is my own mind.

Eventually Ivan came and I had my lesson.

Afterwards, Bev and three other girls came. Bev takes from Francine, who is in a wheelchair because she has lupus. She always waves Bev over when she wants to give her advice. Bev calls her the "Wheelchair Whisperer" and says she is a "high priestess" in her figure-skating religion.

Bev sometimes paints stuff on her cheeks. Like hearts and diamonds. Today it was the number three. I asked why and she said, "It stands for the holy trinity of my religion—my skates, the ice, and me."

I think she wants me to think she's weird. But I don't.

Yours faithfully,

Alice

October 18, 1991

Dear Kristi,

When I came home today, I thought Mom would be in bed as usual, but she was in her studio, sitting in a corner, with her knees bunched into her chest. There was a canvas on her easel. It was smeared with black paint.

She looked tired and her skin had splotches of pink and red, like she'd been swimming in the cold ocean.

She said she tried to paint a picture of the black dog who lives in the yard behind ours.

"Were you painting the dog for Danny?" I asked her.

She said, "It's such a mess."

When I looked in the studio later, I found five canvases smeared with black paint. I thought, It's like falling down on an axel five times in a row.

I'm always thinking about skating. Maybe you've noticed.

Sincerely,

Alice

October 19, 1991

Dear Kristi,

Last night, after Dad came home and I was in bed, I heard my parents talking.

Mom said something about pills and how they weren't making her better, only ruining her art.

Dad said, "You can't paint if you feel like hell."

Mom said, "You don't understand."

They said other stuff, but I stopped listening.

At least Mom doesn't have cancer.

She'll be better soon, right? She always says so when I ask.

A little worried,

Alice

October 20, 1991

Dear Kristi,

I'm preparing for regionals. They're in Columbus, which is two hours from where we live. I'm hoping that since it isn't so far away, Mom will come.

Maybe if I win gold, she'll feel like her old self.

I know: It's like Danny thinking a gold dog will cheer her up.

But I bet your mother will be very, very happy if you win the gold medal at the Olympics.

Sincerely,

Alice

October 21, 1991

Dear Kristi,

Last night I woke up because the black dog was barking like crazy. I thought he must be barking at the moon. Or at the Sherman Strangler.

I heard Mom open her bedroom window. "Stop it!" she yelled at him. "Please, God, stop it!" Eventually, he stopped barking. But afterwards, I heard Mom whisper, "Please, God—stop it! Stop it!"

I must have fallen asleep because when I opened my eyes it was morning.

I don't know if Dad came home last night.

Sincerely,

Alice

October 23, 1991

Dear Kristi,

The Sherman Strangler has been caught! He was the lawyer (public defender) of the women he strangled!

"You don't need the gun anymore," I told Mom.

She said, "I want you to know how much I love you, Alice. You won't forget, will you?"

I said, "Why would I forget?"

She said, "Ever."

I said, "Ever."

I asked Mom if she would come with me to regionals. I want her to see me because, as she told me last year, "We are both artists and we understand each other."

She said, "I really, really wish I could come."

After I left Mom's room, I walked to the rink. I didn't have to worry about the Sherman Strangler, and I didn't see Dad drive by with some woman who isn't Mom. Yippee!

I skated for three-and-a-half hours except for a couple of breaks, so I could warm up my feet in front of the fire. I read four books last week, but all I had in my backpack today was *Anna Karenina*.

Do you know what I want to do before I'm sixteen? Land a triple axel. I know, I know—it's like wanting to win the lottery.

Your ambitious skating friend,

Alice

October 27, 1991

Dear Kristi,

I won regionals!

I can't believe it! I beat Mira Denisovich who is seventeen years old and was born in Moscow!

Ivan was so happy he forgot his English and started talking to me in Russian.

Mom didn't come, but Dad did. Afterward, he said, "We have to celebrate," and he treated Ivan and me to dinner. Dad and Ivan drank a whole bottle of red wine. They toasted each other in eight languages. My father knows a little German, French, Italian, Spanish, and Portuguese. Ivan knows Russian and languages I'm sure he made up.

It was late when we got home from Columbus. Mom was in bed. Dad went to sleep in his study. I tried to sleep in my bed, but I was too excited. I looked out the window and saw the black dog pacing in his yard. I whistled at him, and he stopped and looked up at me. I leaned out the window and showed him my medal. I swear he smiled.

The next morning, Dad was gone and Mom was downstairs with Danny at the breakfast table. Danny was eating a big bowl of Rice Krispies. Mom looked tired, but said, "Congratulations, Alice Marvelous." She wore a blue dress and smelled like flowers.

I asked her if she was going somewhere.

She said, "I have a job interview."

But when Danny and I left to meet the bus, I looked back and Mom was lying on the couch.

Bev picked me up at school. She's driving now! She doesn't think I should have to walk to the rink.

When I showed Bev my medal, she said, "This will be an icon in our church."

I had to ask her what an icon was.

Bev told me her mother wants her to go to an Ivy League college. She said she would rather study mysticism in India. "Or Indiana," she said, and laughed.

Bev's laugh is like an invitation. Even when you don't understand why she's laughing, you still want to laugh with her. I think you would like her.

Yours truly,
Alice

January 10, 1992

Dear Kristi,

I'm sorry I've gone so long without writing to you. My mom died. Well, that's what Dad said I should tell people. If they ask how she died, I'm supposed to say, "She had a serious illness."

But no one at school asks me about her. They all seem to know.

It isn't healthy to think about it, Dad says. So I'll tell the story to you once and never again, okay?

I was in my bed late at night, and I heard a loud sound, like a dog's bark. I wondered if Mom and Dad had bought Danny a dog. So I left my bedroom and walked down the hallway to their room. I said, "Mom? Mom? Did you buy Danny a dog?"

Mom's door was locked from inside with its little hook. I didn't wait for her to come unhook it. I pushed and pushed, and I broke the hook and the door opened.

She was in bed, lying all crooked and wrong. Moonlight covered her. When I saw what had happened to her face, I wanted to scream. But when I opened my mouth, I couldn't make a sound. I rushed out of the room. Danny was in the hallway, saying, "I heard you, Alice. Did they buy me a dog? Did they?"

I couldn't speak.

"I want it now," he said.

I said, "You have to wait, okay? Please?"

He said he didn't want to wait, but he saw my face and said, "Okay, Alice."

I walked him back to his room and watched him climb back into bed.

Dad came up the stairs. He must have been sleeping in his study. He stepped into the bedroom, and I heard him say, "Oh, no. May, please, no!"

Inside the bedroom, he made a phone call. When he stepped outside the room, I was still in front of Danny's room, guarding the door.

Dad looked at me. I said, "I saw."

He covered his face with his hands.

I heard a siren.

January 13, 1992

Dear Kristi,

I forgot to sign my last letter, but I guess it doesn't matter. I haven't mailed you any of them. Obviously.

I didn't go to sectionals. Mom's funeral was the same weekend. Even Ivan understood why I couldn't go.

If I had finished in the top four at sectionals, I would have gone to nationals, where I could have met you. But I probably would have been too shy to say hello.

So I'll say hello now. Hello, Kristi!

I'm trying to be okay. Can you tell? But I think about Mom all the time.

Sincerely,

Alice

January 15, 1992

Dear Kristi,

I haven't gone skating since Mom died. Gran-Gran (Dad's mom) has been with us since the day after she died. We spent Christmas and New Year's at her house in Cleveland.

Gran-Gran drives us to places around town. We spend a lot of time in the Book and Brew, where she buys us ice cream made at the Ohio Eastern Dairy Farm. I am tired of ice cream, but I don't tell her.

Sometimes Gran-Gran will ask if I want to go skating. I always say, "Not today."

Ivan called me and said, "Come back when you want to come back. Tomorrow. Next week. Next month. Next year. I will be here."

Bev called me twice, but I wasn't home. She left messages both times, but I haven't called her back. I don't know what to tell her.

I shouldn't have been at the rink so much. Maybe if I'd stayed home instead of going skating I could have helped Mom.

Sometimes I think it's the Sherman Strangler's fault she's dead. If it hadn't been for the Sherman Strangler, Dad never would have bought the gun.

Sometimes I think it's Dad's fault.

Mostly I think it's my fault. Maybe I'm a devil after all.

I miss her.

Alice

February 1, 1992

Dear Kristi,

Dad bought Danny a dog. It's a one-year-old golden retriever. It's a rescue dog. The people who had the dog before us didn't pay enough attention to it, Dad said. It was lonely, he said.

"Like Mom was lonely?" I said.

"She wasn't lonely," he said.

"She was lonely because you were in love with one of your students," I said. "I saw you."

His face turned red, but for a long time he didn't say anything. "I admit, I am not a saint," he said.

"You're the devil!" I screamed.

Danny started crying, and the dog started barking.

Dad said, "I am not a saint, and I am not the devil. I wish I could have helped your mother more than I did. But she had severe depression. It's an illness, and people can die from it—by doing what she did. I didn't recognize how bad she had it. I should have. I wish I had. I'm so, so sorry."

He started crying. We all started crying.

Afterwards, I wasn't as mad at him anymore.

Sincerely,

Alice

February 21, 1992

Dear Kristi,

Congratulations on winning the Olympic gold medal. I watched you on TV. You skated great. Obviously.

Before we watched the Olympics tonight, Danny and I brought his dog into the backyard. We thought Olympia (I named her!) would bark at the black dog like always. But this time they wagged their tails and sniffed at each other between the fence like they were long lost friends.

And speaking of friends, I think I might give Bev all the letters I've written to you. I'll tell her she can either read them or mail them to you. Did I tell you she sent me roses last week? Her note said, "I miss you in church." She drew two smiley faces in the B of her name.

Sincerely,

Alice

February 22, 2014

Dear Kristi,

I dropped all the letters I've written to you (except this one!) at Bev's house. I left a note with them: "I think I would like you to read these."

Now I'm worried. I hope she doesn't think I'm weird.

I still haven't been to the rink since Mom died.

Sincerely,

Alice

February 23, 1992

Dear Kristi,

Tonight Dad came into my room and said I should go back to skating, to doing what I love.

I said, "If I hadn't skated so much, I could have helped Mom."

I was sitting on my bed. He kneeled down beside it. He has lost a lot of weight and his hair is too long. He put his elbows on my bed and put his hands together like he was praying. He said, "Alice, it isn't your fault, all right? Believe me. Please believe me. There was nothing you could have done."

I said, "I don't believe you."

He said, "I don't know much anymore, but I will always know this: It wasn't your fault. You loved her and she loved you."

I started crying, and he started crying. I put my hands next to his, so we were both praying.

Danny came into the room. When he saw us crying, he started crying. Dad and I both hugged him.

Olympia came into the room and jumped up and down, barking. It was like she wanted to be hugged, so we hugged her until she licked

Danny's ear, and he started squirming on the floor like he was being tickled.

It was so funny we stopped crying.

Sincerely,

Alice

February 24, 1992

Dear Kristi,

Today was my first day back at the rink since Mom died. Bev came up to me and said how sorry she was. So did the other girls.

I didn't want to look at anyone, so I stared at my skates. I guess I felt ashamed and sad. All the girls except Bev skated off. Bev said, "You're a good writer."

"Thank you," I said.

She grabbed hold of both of my hands. "We're going to do a little mourning dance," she said.

"Is this part of your religion?" I asked her.

"Of course," she said.

She led me around the ice. First, she skated backwards, and I skated forwards, then we switched. Then we skated side-by-side like we were ice dancing. I noticed the looks on the other girls' faces. I bet they thought we were crazy.

But I didn't feel crazy. I felt like maybe I'd been in deep, dark water, but had come up for air.

And it was even okay when Bev and I tripped over each other and fell smack on our faces.

"It's one of our sacraments," Bev said, "to kiss the ice."

Both of us kissed the ice and laughed and helped each other up.

Love,

Alice

THE SLEEPING BEAUTY

The sounds in the Sherman Ice Arena are winter. Blades against ice sing like wind across a snow-filled sky. Conversation is as hushed as a landscape of new powder. Sitting in the stands at mid rink, Bill, wearing a heavy black coat, black leather gloves, and a black hat, gazes past the Plexiglas at his seven-year-old granddaughter. Rory, in pink tights, a black sweater, and a black skirt, practices her waltz jumps. The way she leaps—abruptly, with flailing arms, her pony tail smacking against her cheeks like a clapper against a bell—suggests someone who has stepped on a live wire.

Rory reminds Bill of his wife. Barbara loved golf, but she played the game with the herky-jerky motions of a skeleton in a haunted house. Rory resembles Barbara in appearance as well: thin, tall, with black hair (Barbara dyed hers in the last two-and-a-half decades of her life) and prominent cheekbones. They share a big, generous smile. But Rory's laugh is her mother's. Whenever Rory laughs, Bill is reminded of Carol and how he has failed her. At sixty-eight years old, he is running out of time to make everything right.

The heater above him blazes now. He removes his gloves and hat and coat. He looks at his watch, a habit. When he owned Haven's Auto Body, he was forever conscious of the time. To make money, he needed his body men and painters to beat the clock. This became especially imperative in the last few years he owned his business. The insurance companies, having all but eliminated their customers' freedom to choose where their cars were repaired, conducted reverse auctions with the six major collision repair businesses in Sherman. The lowest bidder made money only if he worked with demon speed.

He's retired now. Doubtless the reason Carol thrust Rory on him. This and lack of other options. Rory's father vanished before Rory was born, and Carol isn't in touch with his parents or siblings.

Rory arrived in August, a week before the school year started. Now it's the first week of November. Rory hasn't seen her mother once in this time. She's talked to her on the phone twice. Bill thought Rory would be used to her mother's indifference. But she asks about her frequently, always hopefully.

There are five skaters on the ice besides Rory, all older, and they swirl around her like bees. At Rory's age, Carol liked ballet. Once Bill drove her to Cleveland to see a performance of "The Sleeping Beauty." As he leaned back in his plush seat, contemplating a nap, Carol propped herself on her knees, so she could better see the stage, her face flushed with excitement.

Rory's instructor, Alice Maravicious, as thin and energetic as an exclamation point, hops onto the ice. She does a loop around the rink before gliding up to Rory. Rory's face brightens, her dark eyes suddenly luminous. At the rink, she is alive with eagerness. At school, however, his granddaughter is miserable. Weekday mornings, it's an ordeal to rouse her from bed. Sometimes she'll eat breakfast only to slip back under her covers for another ten minutes of oblivion.

Alice talks to Rory constantly during the lesson, although Bill hears only her warm, encouraging tone. Occasionally, Alice will clap or offer his granddaughter her hand for a high-five. He expected the ice-skating world to be similar to the ballet world he'd left after Carol stopped dancing. Once his daughter had advanced past the introductory classes, she found herself, on the edge of puberty, studying with a pair of Russian émigrés who had left the Siberian winters, but knew how to put a chill in their dancers' confidence.

"You need to challenge yourself," he insisted when she told him she hated the Russians. "They'll make you better."

Instead, they made her miserable and resentful. She was encouraged—told—to quit by one of the Russians, who the same day pulled him aside to say, with her customary inelegance, "She is going nowhere good." He bristled at the insult, but the Russian was right. Alcohol. Drugs. Boys who dropped her off in front of the house in deep hours of the night without seeming to slow down.

He decided she needed both punishment, which included locking her in her room and removing from her possession what she found pleasurable, and verbal correction, which sometimes devolved into yelling. But he was working too hard and too often to enforce his discipline consistently. Meanwhile, Barbara, both because she was afraid of her daughter and because she found her husband's measures too severe, allowed Carol to do as she pleased.

Eventually, Barbara suggested they have Carol see a therapist. Bill balked. Turning Carol over to a therapist—this is how Bill thought of it, as a surrender—would be to admit his failure as a father. At the time, he hadn't heard of manic depression or bipolar disorder. He was waiting on the day—he was sure it would come—when Carol would say, "You were right, Dad. Thank you. Everything is okay now."

Three days before she turned eighteen, Carol left town. He and Barbara, who'd had two miscarriages before Carol's birth, heard from her twice a year, usually when she was drunk or high and crying into a pay phone.

Rory had lived with her mother in a one-bedroom apartment, sometimes sharing it, Rory told him, with her mother's sometimes boyfriends. Carol worked at a bar several blocks from their apartment. She had a hard time waking up in the morning to see Rory off to school. Three months ago, Carol had been sober enough to call Bill and ask him to pick up Rory in Chicago.

Toward the end of her lesson, Rory trips, her body flying— smack—face-forward into the ice. Bill rises, thinking, Hospital. An ankle sprain. A broken nose. Jesus, a concussion. He shuffles to the gate, prepared to march onto the ice. Alice and the other skaters gather around Rory, forming a circle, a cocoon. "Rory," he shouts. "Rory, I'm here." But before he can step onto the ice, he sees Alice pull her to her feet, hears words of solace from the other skaters, hears laughter— Rory's.

Rory returns to her waltz jumps, her blades kissing the ice.

The year after Barbara died, Bill served as president of the Eastern Ohio Auto Body Association. In his twenty-four months in office, he led a crusade against insurance companies' coercive intrusion into the repair business. Antitrust laws forbade him and his associates from price-fixing, but he urged his fellow shop owners to cease offering insurers unsustainable discounts and to stop cutting corners on repairs. But even as they claimed to agree with him, his colleagues petitioned and begged and, in one case he knew, bribed insurers to become their chosen repairers.

Instead of joining them, Bill continued to sound off, dooming his business. Pride cometh before a fall, but he'd foreseen his fall and had proceeded anyway. He'd been fortunate, in the end, to find a buyer for his shop.

"Do you think she'll call me on Saturday?" Rory asks him. They are eating dinner at Ray of Light, a diner in downtown Sherman, where they always eat after her skating lessons.

"I told you I think she will," he says.

"But are you sure?"

He shakes salt onto his French fries. He is about to tell her he is sure, because he knows this will silence her questions. Instead, he says, "I'm sure *I* will call you."

"Why would you call me?" she asks. "We'll be in the same house."

"I'll call you from the next room. I'll shout, 'Happy birthday, Rory.'"

She smiles at this. "I hope she calls," she says, her voice soft.

"So do I."

The waitress, whose name is Dee and who has either a birthmark or a tattoo on the back of her neck, pours him more coffee. Dee, who is in her late fifties, once invited him to a movie. He appreciated her forthrightness, so he accepted. But after the movie, they had trouble making conversation.

"What if none of the people at school come to my party?" Rory asks.

"Somebody'll come. You invited your whole class, didn't you?"

She gives a nearly invisible nod.

"That's twenty-five people. It's almost impossible odds that no one would come."

She bows her head, staring at her hamburger.

He realizes he might be too confident. She's the new kid in her class, after all. He rented the place for Sunday, the day after her birthday. He never would have done this for his daughter. He would have balked at the expense, of course, but also—what? Would he have thought she didn't deserve it?

If he had raised Carol in the opposite way he had, turning every no into a yes, every yes into a no, would she have ended up as she did? Shamefully, he remembers the pleasure he found in his power over her. From her infancy, he crushed her misbehavior, depriving her of what she liked—TV shows, chocolate chip cookies, and, most cruelly, for a week, a stuffed bear she'd had since she was born. He couldn't remember what offense had prompted the latter punishment. She couldn't have been older than five.

At home, after he tucks Rory into bed, he calls Carol. He wants to remind her about Rory's birthday. But her phone rings, and no answering machine picks up. For the next hour-and-a-half, he tries every fifteen minutes, but without success. He falls asleep in his reading chair, phone in hand.

On Friday, at seven in the morning, Bill meets with Rory's teacher. She's meeting with every parent and guardian, and his is the earliest appointment. With her plump cheeks and long, brown ponytail, Beth Downington looks twenty. Sitting in front of her desk, which holds a stack of paperback books, photocopies of multiplication problems, and an apple so red it is certainly fake, Bill feels like a student who is about to be sent to the principal's office.

Ms. Downington hands him Rory's report card. She is good in math, but needs more practice reading aloud. Will he work with her on this? He nods. She shows him an essay Rory has written. It is about her mother, but Bill recognizes it as fantasy. Rory's mother, says the essay, is a professional figure skater and is touring the world. She has gone everywhere—to England, to France, even to the Sahara Desert, where ice, Rory wrote, "lasts only thirty-three minutes."

He considers again his culpability in his daughter's life, wonders furthermore how much responsibility he bears for her failures as a parent. He supposes he might blame his parents for what he became. His father was distant and often absent and, by age forty-six, dead. In order to corral the chaos at home—Bill has five siblings—his mother was strict to the point of severity and, even at four-feet, ten inches, unafraid to discipline her children physically.

"Is she making any friends?" he asks Ms. Downington.

"Slowly," the teacher says. "But I wouldn't say this is unusual. When a new boy comes to school, he's often immediately tested, usually athletically. If he passes the test or proves a good sport about failing it, he finds a place in the group. But for a girl new to a school, the process is slower. And Rory is shy, which makes it harder."

"She's having a party this Sunday. A birthday party. She invited her class."

"She did? Everyone has been remarkably quiet about it."

"On the invitations, I didn't ask parents to RSVP. I hope someone will show up."

"If cake and ice cream are promised..."

"Cake, ice cream, and skating."

"Kids will certainly show up."

After another minute of conversation, he stands to leave. "I imagine I'm the only grandparent looking after his grandchild."

Ms. Downington smiles up at him. "Actually, you're one of three in my class."

"I wonder if we're doing better this time around," he says.

She doesn't appear to understand him.

"Perhaps we were C minus parents, but as grandparents..."

Ms. Downington smiles. "I see," she says. "You're retaking the class."

A pair of faces appears at the window of the classroom, parents waiting their turn. Bill says goodbye and wanders down the hall, which is lined with artwork: handprints, blue silhouettes, a trio of stickmen fishing off the side of a canoe as a whale smiles beneath them. He spots Rory's drawing. It's of an ice skater, of course, one leg lifted parallel to the ice. But the girl isn't alone. There are half a dozen others—smaller, like fairies with skates—around her. They're all smiling, which fills him with unexpected relief.

On Saturday, Carol doesn't call. Before nightfall, he holds off Rory's inquiries with "It's early yet." But at eight o'clock, with Rory buried in her room—she isn't crying, and her silence disturbs him as much as her tears would have—he feels a furious desire to phone his daughter and tell her what a lousy mother she is. But even if he could reach her, he realizes his anger and disappointment would do no good. They never have.

If the best course of action is the opposite of what he is inclined to do, what should he do now?

He rises from the kitchen table, where his coffee has gone cold. His back is stiff. He shuffles off to Rory's bedroom and knocks on her door. When she says nothing, he knocks again. "Rory?" he whispers.

He opens the door and finds her sitting Indian-style on her bed, a doll, dressed in a red skating dress and figure skates, in her hand. Rory moves the doll across the bedspread. She looks up at him, eyes lit with hope. He shakes his head. She twirls her doll.

"The Olympics?" he asks.

"It's only practice," she says. "On a pond." Rory pushes the doll into her bedspread. "Oops, she fell through."

"Is she going to be all right?"

Rory looks up at him. "She'll be wet and cold."

He sits beside her on the bed. A familiar anger boils in him, and he is about to release it in the form of condemnation. Her mother, he will say, is irresponsible, thoughtless, selfish. But this is what the old Bill would have said, and it would do nothing but upset and confuse Rory.

He touches his granddaughter's shoulder, recognizing the stiffness in the gesture. He never found a comfortable way to show Carol affection, perhaps because he didn't often practice.

"I don't think she's able to call you right now," he says.

"Why?" Rory says, her voice neutral. "Is she in jail?"

Bill wonders where Rory came up with this conjecture. "I don't think so," he says. "Not a real jail. But her mind isn't right, and it's like being in a jail. A place you can't escape. A place you can't call from."

Rory is crying now, her head bowed. He hates tears. He sees them as manipulative and melodramatic. He supposes Rory knows this about him, which is why she wipes at them furiously with her forearm. He is about to say, It isn't as bad as all that. Buck up. Pull yourself together.

Do the opposite. "You have every right to be unhappy. Your mother's behavior is confusing. It's hard to forgive what you don't understand."

"I'm ready for bed, Grandpa." Her tears have stopped. Perhaps she is going to save them for when he is gone. He doubts he has been sufficiently comforting. He wonders if in striving to correct past wrongs he's creating a new batch.

"I want to say something to you," he says. Her head is still bowed. She doesn't look up. "Seeing you skate...I haven't told you how impressed I am. It isn't easy. There's always the danger of falling, though I'm sure it helps when you have such nice friends around you, people to pick you up. I wonder if your mother ever had friends like—."

"Mommy's friends are all men with blood in their eyes," she says.

He doesn't know what to say to this revelation. When she looks up, she gives him a soft smile. "Good night, Grandpa."

By 5:30 Sunday afternoon, the hour of her party, no one has shown up. Except for the two of them and Alice, who is doing paperwork in her office, the place is deserted. The ice looks like a plate on which no food has been served. Bill and Rory, in her figure skates, sit in the stands at center ice. He wants to ask her if she handed her classmates the invitations too late. He wants to blame her for this fiasco. In the past, he would have. But he acknowledges the possibility that this is his fault. In his effort to give his granddaughter something nice, something her mother never had, he has, it seems, given her something awful.

He has never been an optimist. Perhaps it's time now to see how it feels. "This is great," he exclaims. "I'm looking forward to eating a lot of birthday cake and watching my favorite skater." He gestures toward the ice. "Go on. Before it melts."

"It won't melt, Grandpa," she says. She steps off the stands and toward the open gate. She looks back at him. "Will it?"

He shakes his head, forcing a smile. She smiles back and glides onto the smooth surface. The public address system crackles, and presently a bright, jaunty piece of music from Rory's favorite movie plays, courtesy of Alice.

He watches Rory skate twice around the rink before moving to the center of the ice to practice her waltz jumps. A profound feeling of loneliness comes over him. He might say it arises out of sympathy for Rory. But it is a familiar loneliness; it often descends on him in early evening, when the sky is helpless against the growing darkness.

"So this is the party?"

Alice stands behind him. In addition to a white sweater and white sweat pants, she wears an enormous white scarf wrapped twice around her neck. She looks like an Arctic angel.

"This is it," he says. He tries to be upbeat.

"Her friends didn't show up?"

"I'm not sure she has any friends," he admits. His words, he fears, sound like an accusation. He isn't angry at Rory, is he? He doesn't blame her. Does he?

"She definitely has friends," Alice says. "Would you like me to see if I can rustle up a few?"

He is about to decline. In Rory's position, he would bristle at charity. He looks at his granddaughter on the ice. She doesn't seem forlorn. But she doesn't seem happy. "If you would," he says. "Thank you."

Alice pulls her cell phone from her sweatpants, punches a button, and brings the phone to her ear.

Twenty minutes later, the ice is populated by a dozen other skaters, swirling around his granddaughter like beautiful birds. He has to fight against a cynical thought: They are here only to take advantage of the free ice. Yet he cannot ignore Rory's smiles and laughter. When two boys of about seventeen, their thighs like cannons, their torsos like barrels, pick her up like a cheerleader and skate with her aloft the entire length of the ice, she produces a sound he might call glee.

Presently, Rory skates between the two boys, holding each one's hand. Occasionally, she jumps into the air, flying across the ice's blue lines and red circles. He recognizes the celebratory music pouring over the public address system. It's from Tchaikovsky's *Sleeping Beauty*.

Perhaps she'll be okay, he concludes of Rory.

But he wonders about Carol, about whether it's too late to help her, to repair whatever bond still exists between them. What if he invited her back home? No, he thinks. No. The old tensions—the anger—the hurt—would resurface. Besides, she would laugh at the idea. This would be the real obstacle—her unwillingness to give him another chance.

But he remembers what Al Harrington, his friend and fellow body shop owner, did when the insurers shunned him. He showed up at every major event in Sherman to hand out goodies with his business's name and phone number on them. Mini-footballs at high-school games, mini-Frisbees at dog shows, key rings at Fourth of July and Veterans Day parades. He became a local celebrity. An event wasn't special if Al wasn't around dispensing lollipops or coffee mugs. Insurers had no choice but to listen to what their customers wanted, and Big Al's Body Works endured. "When the sunlight disappears," Big Al told him, "dance by the light of the moon."

Bill will never have Al's panache, so he'll have to discover a different way to dance. But, watching Rory spin in the center of the party he'd given up as hopeless, he thinks: Maybe I will.

After forty-five minutes, Rory skates to the side of the rink and leaves it through the gate. "I have to pee!" she announces.

"You look like you're having fun," he says.

She wrinkles her forehead as if he could have any doubt. "Of course I am!"

"Look what your classmates are missing." The words are out of his mouth before he can contemplate how they might hurt Rory, remind her of how she has been abandoned.

But she looks at him sheepishly, her cheeks rosy from the cold or embarrassment. "I never invited them, Grandpa."

"You didn't?" he asks. "Why?"

"I didn't want them not to come."

He is still puzzling over her comment, contemplating his granddaughter's pride and her strategy to defeat disappointment—the armor she has built to battle the world, a suit he knows the weight of—when she returns, steps onto the ice, and flies past him, waving.

FIFTY

Marla de León returned home from her disappointing, even outright embarrassing, excursion to the Sherman Ice Arena and strode into her closet, located off the master bathroom, which is to say her bathroom since she was, six months after her divorce, the house's only occupant. Standing in front of her coat rack, she made to remove her overcoat, but noticed how profoundly heavy it was. She struggled, as if in a straightjacket, but seemed about to succeed in casting off her burden when a voice admonished, "Be careful, please." The voice sounded like her mother's. This was disturbing because her mother was dead.

Before she could answer, Marla tumbled to the floor, free of her coat. After she stood up, she turned to face the offending article. Instead of a coat, however, she saw a naked woman. She suppressed a scream only because, although the woman wasn't her mother, she was familiar. Presently, Marla understood why. The woman was herself, a fifty-year-old divorced mother of two and a grandmother—a grandmother!—a designation she'd hadn't fully accepted despite having occupied the role for eight months—of one. Marla might have thought she was looking into a mirror. But the woman's movements did not corresponded with hers. Whereas Marla opened her mouth in disbelief, the woman closed hers in suspicion. "Who the hell are you?" the woman demanded.

"Funny," Marla shot back, "I was about to ask you the same question."

"I live here," the woman said.

"*I* live here," Marla said.

The woman laughed. "Is that so? Where have you been sleeping—in the garage?"

"In my bed," she said. "This bed." She pointed out the door, to the bedroom.

The woman regarded her. "Did you run away from home?" she asked. "Or from boarding school? You couldn't be in college yet, could you?"

I'm as old as you are, Marla thought, but checked herself. This didn't feel true. She pivoted to the full-length mirror where she was shocked to see how youthful she looked. I can't be older than twenty, she thought. She cocked her head to the left, to the right. She batted her eyelashes. She raised her chin. She lowered her chin. She grinned and grinned.

"Wait a minute," said the woman, her outrage apparently overpowering her modesty (she made no effort to cover up). "I know what's going on here. You're trying to ditch me."

Marla was about to answer the woman's accusation with a denial, but the woman was right. A lie, however, seemed the best response—a lie followed by decisive action. "I'm not going to ditch you," she said. But moving faster than she had in thirty years, she shot out of the closet and the attached bathroom before slamming shut the door. Now what? she thought. But the chair in front of the desk in the near corner provided the answer. She grabbed it, returned to the door, and propped the chair under the handle. From within the bathroom came a frustrated groan as her old self, whom she thought of as Fifty, struggled to pull open the door. There was banging. There was kicking. There was cursing.

"You can't do this to me," Fifty shouted. "You can't do this to us."

A sassiness Marla hadn't felt in years surfaced: "I just did."

The chair, which Marla had inherited from her grandmother, might have looked fragile. But whatever wood it was made of—mahogany, redwood, beech—was as durable as concrete.

"We need to talk," said Fifty.

"Later," Marla said.

"You're going to leave me in a bathroom?"

"I'll bring you food in a couple of hours."

"I don't even have anything to read."

"There are clothes in the closet," Marla said. "Read the labels." She paused. "And pick out an outfit. It'll fit."

Feeling as if a weight had been lifted from her, which of course it had, Marla skipped out of the bedroom. To be sure her nemesis remained contained, Marla also propped a chair against the bedroom door.

She looked at her watch. She had left the public figure-skating session at the Sherman Ice Arena twenty minutes after it started. There was time to return.

Marla had grown up in Sherman, had been a member of the Sherman Figure Skating Club, had performed in all of the club's annual shows, including *Alice in Wonderland*, *Cinderella*, and, when a physics professor at Ohio Eastern University with moderate skating talent, but large wallet, had financed the production, to a mash-up of H.G. Wells' *The Time Machine* and *The War of the Worlds*. Now, after minutes on the ice, she'd felt brittle and twice as old as she was. She absorbed the stares of the other skaters—teenagers on awkward first dates, young children in safety helmets and their bored parents, twins in pink skating dresses doing side-by-side, identical spirals as if in a TV ad for Doublemint gum—all of them doubtless wondering why a fifty-year-old woman was spending her Friday night performing torturous half loops and enervated scratch spins at center ice. She imagined their mockery pouring on her like ice water. So she'd fled, disgraced.

She looked at her watch again. There was more than an hour of ice time left. Her return, at once half an hour later and thirty years earlier, would be nothing less than triumphant.

The couples therapist Marla and Dave had seen in Baltimore, where they'd lived for twenty-eight years prior to moving back to Sherman the previous January, believed Dave was experiencing a mid-life crisis. He and Marla were heading with alarming speed toward their twenty-fifth wedding anniversary and fiftieth birthdays. If Dave's mid-life anxieties could be channeled into relatively tame extravagances, such as sports cars or powerboats, the marriage could be saved, the therapist said. If as remedy he sought the company of women, he risked exploding it.

Dave's job as a cardiologist at Johns Hopkins offered him ample opportunity for extramarital adventure. Early in their marriage, he'd had an affair with an emergency-room nurse, a transgression he tearfully confessed to Marla and which she forgave. There may have been other betrayals to which he hadn't confessed. But he seemed sincere about fighting off his midlife demons, which is why their return to their hometown had been so promising. He had been offered a job as chief of cardiology at Ohio Eastern University Hospital. They would resurrect their relationship in the place it had been born.

When, three months into their return, Dave reconnected with his high school girlfriend, she wasn't worried. The woman, Greta, was dying of esophageal cancer, and Dave's pilgrimages to her bedside seemed to Marla nostalgic rather than romantic. What she hadn't foreseen was the presence of Greta's twenty-seven-year-old daughter at her mother's bedside. A month after Greta's death, Dave asked Marla for a divorce so he could marry the woman Marla soon referred to as Greta Fucking Junior.

At the Sherman Ice Arena, Marla held center ice like a master magician holds the stage. The teenagers and parents who previously had cast disdainful and pitying gazes her way now stared at her with amazement. Marla's performance was all the more stunning because she was using rental skates. What she could have done with a pair of Kristi Yamaguchi-endorsed, titanium-bladed Riedell figure skates!

As the night grew later, the crowd changed. Families departed, college students arrived. A disco ball descended from the scoreboard above center ice, spraying blue, red, and green light around the rink. What would fifty-year-old Marla think of such a display? Twenty-year-old Marla didn't know. But twenty-year-old Marla loved it. She spun, she jumped, she did a shoot-the-duck from one end of the rink to the other, drawing a warning from one of the skate guards to "Be careful. Skating blades are like knives."

Back at center ice, she caught the eye of a young man in an Ohio Eastern sweatshirt whose hair was a swirl of blond and brown and whose chin had the straight edge of a guillotine. He wasn't the most elegant skater, but he was fearless, whirling around her like a storm.

When Marla returned to her house, it was nearly three in the morning. She discovered Fifty on the closet floor, sleeping, her snores as loud as fog horns. Is that what I sound like? Marla wondered, appalled. She opted against waking the woman, but Fifty, dressed in pajamas, cracked open her eyes. "You smell like beer," she said. "And cigarettes."

"I went out after ice skating," Marla said.

"With whom?"

"Friends."

"All of our friends go to bed before ten."

"All of *your* friends go to bed before ten. These are new friends."

"Do tell."

So Marla did, sanitizing the part in which she and Kevin, the blond-brown from the rink, found themselves sharing a bottle of vodka and each other's lips in a basement somewhere in Partytown, Sherman's student-dominated neighborhood.

"Sounds fun," Fifty concluded.

"It was."

"I'm hungry."

"Oh," Marla said and realized that she, too, was hungry. "I'll make us something."

With apologies, Marla locked up Fifty again and found her way to the kitchen. She hadn't become a serious cook until her children were born, and, because this hadn't yet happened, she discovered she knew only the bare fundamentals. Indeed, she remembered only the outlines of her life after age twenty. She returned to Fifty carrying two bowls of out-of-a-box mac and cheese.

After her first bite, Fifty shivered. "You've overcooked the noodles," she said, "and this cheese mix tastes like gun powder."

"Bang, bang," Marla said, although after she ate a forkful, she understood the criticism. But she was hungry enough to eat it all. Fifty didn't feel the same compulsion.

"Why don't you let me cook next time?" Fifty said.

Marla sensed a ruse. If she allowed Fifty out of her prison, who knew what she might do. Her biggest worry was being reunited, in a single body, with the old woman.

"Next time, I'll order in," Marla said. She grabbed Fifty's bowl and stepped out of the closet.

"Could you at least loan me a pillow?" Fifty asked.

"You can have the whole bedroom," Marla said. When she invited Kevin to the house, she wouldn't want him anywhere near Fifty. Marla would make use of the guest bedroom in the basement. After she left the master bedroom, she propped the chair under the door handle. "Sweet dreams," she said to the closed door.

"I could make us breakfast tomorrow," Fifty said. "Eggs, bacon, pancakes."

"I'll think about it," Marla said.

"A gun?" Fifty asked incredulously. It was lunchtime a week later.

"How else am I going to be sure you stay put?" Marla shot back.

"Where'd you even get it?"

"Kevin."

"What does he need with a gun? He's a college student."

"He's on the rifle team."

"And the rifle team has started using Saturday Night Specials?"

"He's worried about crime in his neighborhood," Marla said.

"He lives in Partytown," Fifty said. "The only crime he's likely to see is a drunk college kid pissing on his lawn."

"He doesn't have a lawn," Marla admitted. "Okay, maybe he has a gun fetish. I don't know."

"Does he have tattoos?"

"Who are you?" Marla shot back, exasperated. "My mother?"

"Worse. I'm you plus thirty years."

"He's sexy. In bed, he's even sexier."

"I hope you're using proper protection."

"Like you did when you were my age?"

This silenced the older woman. After a moment, she said, "So you're going to set me free?"

"In order to make lunch. If I have to eat one more slice of pizza, I'm going to barf."

"So I'll be cooking with a gun to my head."

"I'll only use it if you try anything suspicious."

"Like what? Experimenting with oregano?"

They stepped into the kitchen. Three bags of groceries were piled on the counter. "I didn't really know what to get," Marla said, "except for chocolate."

"My favorite," Fifty said. "*Our* favorite, I suppose."

"I got a little of everything. Chicken, vegetables, fruit, bread, and a bottle of mouthwash."

"I could use some floss," Fifty said.

"I never floss."

"Which is why I need to."

"Oh. Well, I've run out of cash."

"It happens when a person doesn't have a job."

"You'll have to tell me the pin number of your ATM card."

"You don't remember?"

"No," Marla admitted.

Fifty smiled. "I'm not telling you."

Marla waggled the gun at the older woman. "I never thought I'd threaten myself with a gun," she said. "But here I go." In as stern a voice as she could muster, she said, "Give me the goddamn PIN."

"Or...?"

"Or I'll shoot you."

"Which would be a kind of suicide, wouldn't it?"

"I don't know what it would be."

"And you still wouldn't have the PIN."

"You're willing to die over a PIN?"

"I'm not sure I'm even alive." Fifty paused. "Or maybe I'm half alive."

"What do you mean?" Marla asked. It was a serious question. Ever since she'd freed herself from her fifty-year-old body, she'd had the feeling that something was missing.

"Some of the old impulses—relating to eating, drinking, and being merry—have diminished, replaced by a somewhat disconcerting absence of longing," Fifty said. "I feel older than fifty; I feel more like eighty. It's as if I gained the years you lost."

"Sorry," Marla said, although she wasn't.

"I feel like a Buddhist. Or a ghost." She tapped her finger against her lips. "I can't say I'm unhappy about it. It's just…well…new."

Marla smiled. "So we're both loving life."

"You're loving life," Fifty said. "I'm beginning to relish the absence of desire." She looked past Marla, a peaceful look on her face, before gazing at her again. "I think the two of us should work together."

"Explain."

"We each have certain skill sets. I know how to cook, hold down a job, run a house. You know how to skate like an angel, attract the attentions of virile young men, and sleep until noon. But in order to function fully, I need to move about without a gun trained at my head."

"I don't trust you."

"Why?" Fifty asked.

"Because the whole reason I am who I am is because I didn't want to be who you are."

"Which means what?"

"Which means when I drop my guard, you'll jump me and we'll be one person again."

"Perhaps I didn't make this clear: I like who I am. To no longer want to land a double axel? To no longer crave a man who I imagine would offer stimulating conversation and a medley of orgasms, but proves borderline psychotic or, worse, boring? One word: freedom. Freedom from want! What a joy!"

"I still don't believe you."

"Why?"

"Because I can't imagine ever wanting to give up figure skating or fucking."

"I didn't say I wanted to give up either. I said the desire to do both no longer consumes me."

Marla sighed.

"Still don't believe me?" Fifty asked.

"I'm hungry," Marla said.

"Let me fix us a meal. We'll talk afterwards."

Fifty's meal was splendid, and Marla responded to it the way she did sometimes long ago to splendid, filling meals: She fell asleep at the table.

When she awoke, Fifty was gone. Of course she was. Marla wondered if the old woman had put Dramamine in her meal. Or perhaps the witch had simply cast a spell. She stomped around the house in a fury. But after a minute of loud petulance, Marla realized the situation could have been worse—far worse. Fifty could have pounced on her, unifying them again.

A few minutes later, Fifty returned. She had gone to the ATM. She slid $20 across the kitchen counter to Marla. Marla's happiness at seeing the old woman return was tempered by her graying counterpart's stinginess. "Is this it?" Marla wanted to say. But she checked herself. If she needed money later, she would slip it out of Fifty's wallet.

"The afternoon is all yours," Fifty said.

"Great!" Marla said. There was a freestyle session at the skating rink. Afterwards, she was supposed to meet Kevin, although he'd been vague about the time and location. It didn't matter. She was young; she could be casual.

"Kevin Peterson is the boy you're dating, correct?" Fifty asked her.

Marla looked at the old woman suspiciously before nodding. "Do you know him?"

"I know of him. He's the younger brother of the woman who is now our—my—ex-husband's wife."

"Is this a problem?"

"For me? No."

"What about for me?"

"I would hate to prejudice your feelings toward him."

"What do you mean? Do you know something?"

"It's nothing," Fifty said. "As you said, I'm not your mother."

"Come on. Tell me."

"I won't tell you." Fifty looked at her with what, shockingly, was sympathy. "But if I had a few words of advice, they would be: Guard your heart."

Fifty was right. Kevin broke her heart—and quickly. Three weeks after her conversation with the old woman, Marla discovered Kevin's secret: He was in a long-term relationship with a junior at St. Mary's College in Cleveland. She was, Marla deduced, the virgin he aspired to marry. He'd taken her to the Valentine's Ball at Ohio Eastern. For several days preceding the ball, Marla had pestered him to take her. Finally, frustrated with her lobbying, he had admitted the truth. She called him a two-timing asshole. He accepted her criticism with a shrug. "My door's always open to you," he added.

"Well, my door is locked and bolted," Marla replied.

When Marla returned home, she sobbed at the kitchen table as Fifty offered consolation in the form of strawberry-banana crepes with a chocolate garnish.

Toward the end of the night, Fifty gazed at her with pity and said, "I should be envious of you. Your youth. Your beauty. But I wouldn't trade places with you right now even if on top of your beauty and youth, I inherited an Italian villa."

Marla's eyes remained tear-filled. "You wouldn't?" she asked pitifully.

"But only because the one time I went to Italy I became so constipated on pasta I had to drink a 32-ounce bottle of prune juice to remedy the situation."

Marla tried to smile. When she failed, Fifty smiled for her. "I'd like to say it gets better," Fifty said.

"Why don't you?"

"Because it wouldn't be true."

Marla eyed her. "Are you just saying that?"

"What do you mean?"

"Saying that it won't get better because you're jealous and you want me back?"

Fifty smiled again. "Do I look like I'm jealous and want you back?"

Marla considered the old woman's face. It wore all of her fifty years and more. Even so, its serenity made it attractive and appealing—beautiful even.

"Even if romance fails," Fifty said, "you always have figure skating."

"Yes, I do," Marla said, although with less conviction than she'd wanted.

Two days later, Fifty returned from a trip to Cleveland with a pair of Kristi Yamaguchi-endorsed Riedell figure skates with titanium blades.

"How did you know my size?" Marla asked, but immediately she knew, and both women laughed.

They were superb skates, and the next time Marla was on the ice, during a freestyle session, she moved and spun and jumped like an aspiring Olympian. Only one of the nine other figure skaters on the ice complimented her. The rest gave her envious glances and worked harder on their axels and lutzes. She shouldn't have expected anything else. She knew this world; if friendship existed among figure skaters, it was inevitably among figure skaters of widely different abilities. Nevertheless, she felt an overpowering loneliness. It wasn't unfamiliar, yet it hit with the force of revelation. She skated to the end of the rink and stared up at the scoreboard's large digital clock, clicking off the seconds. She wondered when Fifty had stopped skating seriously. Might this, she wondered, have been the moment she quit?

But what would I do without skating? she wondered.

She answered: College. Or a job.

But neither seemed desirable. Or, rather, they seemed to require from her a commitment she wasn't prepared—or prepared yet—to make. She wondered what Fifty had done when she was twenty. Marla should know—it was her history, after all. No, it was her future, and it was a mystery.

For several weeks, she returned to freestyle sessions at the Sherman Ice Arena, something Fifty encouraged her to do, but the pizzazz was gone. She spent public skating sessions within the circle of orange cones at center ice, spinning like a ballerina on a speeded-up music box and hoping to impress whoever drifted, stumbled, staggered, and sometimes even skated by. After her disaster with Kevin, however, men of her age at the rink seemed unappealing and immature. Sometimes as she skated, Marla scanned the bleachers behind the Plexiglas to see if there was a divorced father who, glancing up from his laptop or newspaper, might catch her eye. She decided she might even settle for a married man, someone who could at least show her a good time. If she sounded desperate, it was because she had shed thirty years specifically to be thrilled, and she found the gap between what she'd desired and what she'd discovered confounding and frustrating.

Compounding her feelings of loneliness and desperation was the contrast between her life and Fifty's. Fifty, who made a living as a freelance technical writer and editor, attended public lectures at Ohio Eastern University several nights a week. The topics ranged from global warming to "The Art of Cilantro." She'd also enrolled in a Chinese language class.

Marla tried to express enthusiasm for Fifty's life—the old woman had been good to her, after all—but it was a struggle. She found herself examining Fifty with envy, noting how she seemed less old every day, seemed to be enjoying a renaissance not only of spirit but of body. By contrast, whenever Marla looked in the mirror, she saw a puffiness that suggested more than her recent uninhibited devouring of Fifty's meals and her post-midnight raids on what the two women had dubbed "the chocolate cupboard." It spoke of weariness and disappointment and an ungraceful move from youth to maturity.

She knew there were better remedies to her blue mood than drinking, than drugs, than boys. But these were the most accessible. One night, it was Henry with a six-pack and marijuana. Another night, it was James with bourbon and painkillers. A third night, it was Eddie with vodka and cocaine. The basement bedroom resonated with her lonely debauchery. Fifty didn't complain about the unseemliness of her behavior, but over meals she did eye Marla with unmistakable compassion. Marla might have felt patronized if she didn't believe Fifty's concern was sincere.

Intuitively, Marla recognized a danger in appearing unhinged and at loose ends, although she thought the consequences would be no direr than a stern lecture from her older self. Over dinner one night, she tried to be upbeat in Fifty's presence. But she'd never been much of an actress, and by the time Fifty served chocolate pie with chocolate ice cream, her expression had fallen. I wanted this life, she thought, although her reasons—to skate brilliantly, to dazzle boys with her beauty—seemed less the fantasies of a middle-aged woman than of a twelve-year-old girl.

One night, she brought home Mike, a 19-year-old she'd met at the rink. He was so drunk on Sherman Slammer, the local moonshine, that he collapsed in the foyer of the house before he could remove his shoes. To compound the disaster, he peed his pants, his urine soaking through Fifty's Guatemalan rug and onto the white carpet. As he lay unconscious, Marla picked up a letter opener off a nearby bookshelf and fantasized about driving it into his neck. Instead, she imitated slashing it across her wrist. There must be a better way, she thought.

Although the answer presented itself quickly, she at first resisted. It seemed to her the equivalent of heading off on a safari only to reach an impassable section of trail and, with fantasies of seeing tigers and lions crushed, turning back, defeated. But she could see no alternative.

The next afternoon, Fifty invited her into the master bedroom in order to show her the dress she planned to wear on her evening date.

"What date?" Marla asked.

"He's a professor of art history," Fifty said, posing in front of her floor-to-ceiling mirror. "I've attended three of his lectures. After each, he asked me on dates. Third time was the charm."

Fifty glowed like a firefly, her aura so strong it projected light in all directions. It wasn't fair, Marla decided, that in freeing herself from Fifty, she'd made the old woman happy. It was supposed to work the other way.

Now? Marla wondered of her plan.

Now, she decided, but Fifty said, "Hold on a minute. I bought new earrings. I left them in the living room."

She stepped out of the bedroom and shut the door. Presently, Marla heard a familiar sound.

"Are you putting a chair against the door?" Marla asked. She turned the handle but the door didn't budge. "Let me out!"

"It won't be permanent," Fifty said. "But I know what you're thinking."

"How do you know?"

"Because I've been you!"

Although Marla continued her protest, she suspected Fifty had left the house. Marla immediately thought of the window. If a fifty-year-old woman might hesitate to jump from the second floor, a twenty-year old, with less brittle bones, wouldn't think twice about it—unless there was something below the window to deter her. Which there was. Fifty, old but wise, had decorated the landing spot with shovels, knives, pitchforks, and other assorted tools, weapons, and utensils. Marla might have cursed if her anger hadn't been superseded by admiration. I will be this smart one day, she thought.

She considered other ways to escape. She contemplated chipping a tunnel in the drywall, but Fifty had removed from the bedroom any items that might serve to break down the walls, including several old figure-skating trophies. The best Marla had was a hairbrush. She fantasized about removing the toilet and escaping via sewer pipes. Or, barring this, flushing a message, protected in a ziplock bag (of which she had a single one), down the toilet and hoping someone might discover it and free her.

Days passed, and although Marla couldn't complain about the meals Fifty served her, nor about much of anything else—Fifty fed her copies of *People* and *US Weekly* and even installed an exercise bicycle in the bedroom—she'd had enough of her unsettled youth. She wanted serenity, stability, freedom from the intense and wild demands of her heart and libido and the downward pull of depression. She wanted to be Fifty.

Weeks into Marla's captivity, Fifty, despite mild protestations to the contrary, didn't seem any closer to releasing her. It was essential, therefore, for Marla to act on a plan she'd recently conceived, although if she failed, she might never have another opportunity.

To pass the time, Marla indulged in frequent baths, a practice Fifty criticized, albeit mildly, because of the water bill. In addition to using the baths as boredom breakers and relaxation inducers, Marla employed them as a practice ground for the execution of her plan. A dozen times during a bath, she slipped under the water and held her breath for as long as she could. Initially, she could manage only twenty-five seconds. But after a couple of weeks, she was pushing two minutes. After a month, she was a submarine.

Fifty was a woman of routine, and this worked to Marla's advantage. She knew to draw her bath five minutes before six p.m., immediately before Fifty marched into the room with her dinner. In order to ascertain that Marla was nowhere near her when she stepped into the room, Fifty insisted that Marla sing to her from afar. Today, Marla, who'd stripped in preparation for her bath, sang from the edge of the tub. The song was "Reunited," which Marla realized only after she started was a hint of her intentions. Thankfully, Fifty didn't seem to notice.

The bathroom door was open, so the two women could see each other. Fifty placed Marla's dinner at the foot of the bed. "Enjoy," she said, which is what she always said.

"I'll eat after my bath," Marla said, and she slipped into the tub—literally slipped. "Oh!" she exclaimed as her feet slid out from under her. She was under water, on her back, gazing up like a zombie. She started counting in her head like she did when she practiced.

Fifty didn't charge into the bathroom as Marla had hoped. Marla wondered if the old woman had left the bedroom already, oblivious to the staged tragedy unfolding in the bathtub. She considered surfacing and implementing her plan another day. But she waited, and she was rewarded seconds later when Fifty appeared above her, a watery blur of gray hair and concern. Fifty said nothing, and although Marla couldn't make out the woman's features, she guessed she was scrutinizing her, worried about a trick.

Perhaps ten seconds ticked past, and Marla felt the first throbs of desire to breathe. In lockstep with her blossoming panic was a feeling of incredulity: Was Fifty really going to let her drown? If this was the case, she had underestimated the woman's—and her own future— compassion. Or perhaps Fifty knew exactly how many seconds a brain could be deprived of oxygen before permanent damage set in. How long could this be? Marla wondered. Two minutes? Ten minutes? Half an hour?

She couldn't last much longer.

Marla heard Fifty's words, garbled as if over a bad connection: "This isn't a trap, is it? Please swear to me it isn't a trap."

But if Marla swore it wasn't a trap, she would in fact be admitting it was a trap. She continued to gaze, zombie-like, up into the woman's looming face, the desire to breath becoming progressively overwhelming. She thought briefly of springing from the bath, as a woman had done in a horror movie she'd seen, but she suspected Fifty would be prepared for such an assault and would evade it. No, she had to stick with the plan: She needed the old woman to come to her.

Two minutes must have passed, and Marla wondered if it was possible she could, in fact, die, black out and die, as her suspicious older self looked down. If she died, would Fifty die? Or would she remain as she was now, stripped of the young portion of her, absent its life-affirming but life-confusing energy? Perhaps Fifty was debating this very concern. Deciding she could give herself only ten seconds more, Marla began an urgent countdown in her head. *Ten, nine, eight...*Fifty continued to gaze down at her from godly heights...*Seven, six, five...*"I've seen *Fatal Attraction*," Fifty mumbled. "Please don't let this be a sequel."...*Four, three, two...*Marla wondered if it would have been better to wish to return at a different age. Thirty-one, thirty-two, thirty-three—they were the real golden era, weren't they? And her tenth year had been delightful, she believed, although her depleted brain would admit no memories of this time...*One.*

Suddenly, Fifty's face was suspended inches from hers, as if through a watery window. Marla felt the old woman's hands reach under her arms and draw her up. At the same time, Marla reached for Fifty, looping her arms around her waist. Marla had gravity and strength on her side, but Fifty had craftiness. She tickled Marla's armpits. The sensation was so shocking she nearly lost hold of the old woman. But she held on, and Fifty crashed into her. Their embrace was half a dance, half a wrestling match. Eventually, it was a coupling more intimate than sex.

The water rose around them before rolling into a wave and spitting them out of the tub as if onto a shore. By now, it was hard to determine who was who as they had mostly merged into one body, but somebody said, "I want," and somebody else, or the same person, repeated, "I want," and there was laughter undercut by tears, or the inverse. Even before she crawled to the closet, to the mirror, she knew who she was, although she wondered about the value of such wisdom when she couldn't recall, though she now wanted to, desperately, what chocolate had tasted like the very first time.

DUETS

From the top of the three-tier bleachers, Danielle squints across the cloud-white ice, where a faint mist rises, and imagines that the five-year-old girl moving across it isn't her daughter but herself, three decades ago. It is easy to do: Danielle learned how to skate in this very rink.

She started off in group lessons, but by the time she turned seven, she had a private instructor, Joe Greicius, who was tall, slim, and foreboding, like a prehistoric bird. He must have been at least six-feet, four, and of course his skates made him seem even taller. His voice was deep and resonant, echoing off the boards around the rink, and he smelled of tangerine cologne and fresh-cut ice. When he smiled at her, his dimples framing a soft mouth, she never failed to blush.

Joe was from a country in Eastern Europe (she'd forgotten which), and his accent was pronounced. He was often stern with her, letting her know when her spirals and waltz jumps and, later, her lutzes and axels, were flawed. But at the end of every lesson, he offered her his hand to shake and said, with enthusiasm, "You do very well, Danny girl."

The girls on the ice are all outfitted in bike helmets—two pinks, one orange, one green—and Alice, their instructor, encourages them, in a voice as light and enthusiastic as a bird's greeting the sunrise, to spread their arms and walk toward her. They are learning their balance, and two of the girls tumble immediately. Danielle's daughter, Natalie, and the other pink-helmeted skater remain on their feet all the way to Alice, who applauds their success, then retrieves the fallen girls from the ice.

The mother of the other skater in pink, who shares her daughter's red hair, sits on the first tier of bleachers. When Danielle catches her glance, she introduces herself. The woman does the same, adding, "I have a feeling I know you."

At thirty-six, Danielle looks like she did in college, pencil thin, her black hair cut, as her hairdresser describes it, "short and smart." She flatters herself to think she might, on first inspection, anyway, be mistaken for a European model or one of the waif-like actresses who dominated Hollywood a decade before. She inherited her looks from her mother, although her mother's beauty was bolder—bigger and redder lips, thicker and darker hair, legs so long and comely she'd once been recruited to model for a Cleveland department-store catalogue—even as she did little, by way of makeup or clothes, to emphasize it.

Obligingly, Danielle provides the woman, Samantha, her history: She moved to Sherman with her daughter in the summer. Prior to this, she lived in several cities, which she names with fondness but also a rueful finality, the same way she speaks of her ex-lovers. Samantha frowns. "I wasn't in any of those places," she says. Until she was twenty-six, Samantha skated in the Ice Capades. When it folded, she found work in public relations. For the last three years, she has worked in the marketing department at Ohio Eastern University.

"Maybe I look like someone you know," Danielle offers. Samantha smiles and says, "Probably so."

Alice marches in front of her students. They are supposed to copy her, but only Natalie and Samantha's daughter, Lil, manage to do so with any grace. One of the girls clings to the boards. The other stands as if paralyzed.

"You didn't want to teach your daughter how to skate?" Danielle asks Samantha. "You obviously have the know-how."

Samantha smiles. "I'm too impatient. Whenever I see her struggle, I'm reminded of myself at her age. Always a little slow, a little dreamy."

"But if you were in the Ice Capades, you must have been a star."

"I wasn't one of the principal skaters. I was in the equivalent of the company." She pauses. "But the travel, the people I met, what I learned—I had a great time. And now here I am, back in my hometown."

"You grew up here?"

Samantha nods. The red hair. Was it possible? "So you learned to skate here?" Danielle asks.

"Sure did."

"I did too."

"No kidding."

Danielle leans forward. She catches the smell of the ice. Its associations are pleasant and comforting. "You didn't happen to take lessons from Joe Greicius, did you?"

"Wait," Samantha says. "I know who you are. You're Danny!"

"And you're the little red-headed girl who used to take lessons after I did."

"I remember when you and your family left town."

Danielle and her family lived in Sherman until she was ten, when her father, a history professor at Ohio Eastern, was hired at the University of Illinois at Springfield. Four years after their move, her mother was diagnosed with breast cancer. It hadn't been caught early, and the treatment—almost primitive in its brutality, the way it punished her body—made her death seem less a tragedy than a pardon from pain.

But of course Danielle hadn't wanted her mother to die, no matter her agony. For months afterward, Danielle felt she *hadn't* died, that she might turn a corner in their house and find her mother, as she used to, on the couch in the corner of the living room, a book in her lap, Bessie Smith or Billie Holiday playing on the record player. This time, Danielle vowed, she wouldn't bow to her mother's desire to be alone. She would slip next to her, and if she couldn't convince her to tell her about what she was reading, she would be content to listen to the same music. But of course she always found the living room empty and silent.

Danielle didn't return to Sherman out of nostalgia. After her divorce, she needed a position with benefits. She works in medical records at University Hospital. She has never had a career; instead, she has moved from job to job like a bee to flowers. Even in college, she couldn't focus on a particular path. She graduated with a degree in general studies. Her aimlessness was acceptable when she was married because her ex-husband, a patent lawyer, had a solid career. But now she wonders what she's doing with her life.

"So you were obviously dead serious about skating," Danielle says.

"Not at first," Samantha says. "My parents insisted I keep with it. I think they were worried I would become a drunk or a drug addict if I didn't have structure in my life." She laughs at her joke. "But eventually, when I became halfway decent at it, I started to like it—love it, in fact. What about you?"

"I gave it up." Her lessons with Joe Greicius stopped abruptly. Afterwards, she briefly tried ballet. But in the year or so between stopping skating and leaving Sherman for Springfield, she mostly holed up in her room and read and listened to music. It was an especially quiet time in her house, which was no stranger to silence. In answer to why her skating lessons stopped, her parents said they were becoming too expensive. When she protested, her father said, with a grimness she knew not to contradict, "It's good to explore your other talents."

When they moved to Springfield, her father asked her if she wanted to skate again. But he didn't seem enthusiastic about the prospect, and, wanting to please him, she declined.

"I remember how good you were," Samantha says. "I would come ten minutes before my lesson—my mother was uber-punctual—and stand right here and watch you." She points to the Plexiglas in front of her. "I worried I would never be as good as you."

Danielle *was* good. Whatever had been quiet and restrained in her at home and at school, she unleashed on the ice. She fell down all the time, but this was good, said Joe Greicius, because it showed she was pushing herself to be better. "The skater who never falls down," he said, "is a bird who will never fly."

"Why did you stop?" Samantha asks her.

Danielle thinks to mention how expensive lessons were. But her father had been a named professor. He had no income-sucking habits, his gambling limited to driving through yellow lights and his drinking restricted to the coffee he consumed by the pot. Her father might have been frugal, but he wasn't capricious. He wasn't someone who, suddenly concerned about the household budget, a budget in no danger of bursting, would pull her from something she loved. Her parents didn't stop her brother's saxophone lessons, after all.

"I don't know," Danielle says. "I liked skating. I liked it a lot."

It was always her mother who brought her to the rink, sitting in the stands she sits in now. Sometimes she brought a book. Sometimes she would gaze out at the rink, her expression unreadable. After her lessons, her mother conferred with Joe Greicius in front of the fireplace in the lobby. Danielle would drift off to a far corner of the room, where there was a pinball machine. She never had a quarter to play, but she would snap the ball release and gaze at the flashing red, silver, and blue lights.

After one of her lessons, Joe invited her mother onto the ice. He said it would be easier to explain what he was teaching Danielle if he could also teach it to her. As far as Danielle knew, her mother had never skated. It surprised her, therefore, when her mother, who was two inches shy of six feet, her stature enhanced by her thinness, proved agile and adept, sometimes skating beside Joe, as if the two were walking in the park, sometimes skating backwards but in front of him, their hands clasped in a duet.

If Joe showed her mother anything Danielle had been learning, Danielle failed to recognize it. She was, instead, struck by the rare liveliness in her mother's eyes and, even rarer, the way she sometimes tossed her head back and laughed.

"What happened to Joe Greicius, anyway?" she asks Samantha. "Is he still around?"

"He left town maybe four years after you did," Samantha says. "Of course I was devastated. All the girls were. And their mothers!" She laughs.

"Their mothers?"

"He was handsome, didn't you notice? And he was charming the way someone who doesn't speak English well can be charming. You want to hug him even as you're mentally correcting his grammar."

"Was he married?"

"No, but he moved to Cleveland and married another Lithuanian, someone right off the boat." Samantha covers her mouth, removes her hand. "I hope that doesn't sound insensitive. He became a weatherman on one of the Cleveland channels. I don't know how that happened. We used to see his newscast down here sometimes. He still didn't speak great English, but his charm remained."

"He's still in Cleveland?"

"Los Angeles, last I heard."

"Still a weatherman?"

"It can't be a difficult job in L.A." She grins. "Smog and heat, smog and heat."

Danielle notices the cold. The heater above them has clicked off.

Did her father ever come to see her skate? He must have. She'd been in competitions in Cleveland and Columbus; she'd participated in all the local shows, mini-holiday showcases and *Cinderella on Ice*, hosted by the Sherman Figure Skating Club. But during their last years in Sherman, her father embarked on a giant project on the Civil War, intending to write a day-by-day history of the entire April-1961-to-April-1965 conflict. His named professorship allowed him time to travel to battlefields from Gettysburg to Vicksburg to Chickamauga.

Her father was a decade older than her mother, but he could seem younger, becoming whiny and worried when he couldn't find his glasses or a book he needed and sullen, even sulky, when he failed to receive an award or a grant. But if Danielle saw her mother more than her father, her father was more approachable, more knowable. From a young age, she recognized his flaws—his insecurity, his anxiety—and tolerated them as a necessary counterbalance to his strengths, which could be summed up as kindness. He made her school lunches, and, until she was well into middle school, always included a note, sometimes a quotation from a Civil War general, sometimes a joke, but usually his own sweet words.

Her mother's moods—or mood (she seemed to have only one)—were difficult to read. Serenity? Boredom? Or was her face a Zen-like mask to cover unhappiness? Danielle remembers a Mother's Day at the height of her figure-skating infatuation. As a gift, she'd painted her mother a picture of the two of them skating on a frozen lake, although, sloppily, she'd depicted her mother, angel-like, elevated above the ice. To Danielle's and her brother's presents—he'd recorded a cassette tape of his original, dreadful saxophone solos—her mother smiled but only in the way she might smile at a neighborhood cat she'd seen playing in dandelions from the kitchen window. Danielle would have been disappointed if she had expected a different reaction.

This was why when her mother laughed as she skated with Joe Greicius, Danielle felt unsettled, as if a door she'd stood in front of a thousand times but knew was locked had suddenly opened. She wondered why it couldn't have been she who opened it.

"I think my mother was one of the mothers he charmed," Danielle tells Samantha.

Samantha turns to her, gives her a quick smile. "And she was worth charming, as I recall. Wasn't she some kind of Victoria's Secret model before Victoria's Secret existed?"

Danielle shrugs, says, "Kind of." They turn back to the ice, where Alice has set up a game of Sharks and Minnows. It isn't fair: Natalie and Lil skate past the other girls as if they are statues.

Danielle's father, in his late seventies now, is remarried and living in Dallas. Although she speaks to him twice a month, she can't ask him if her mother had an affair with Joe Greicius. They don't have this kind of relationship. And Danielle isn't about to look up Joe's phone number in Los Angeles or find him on Facebook with the intention of discovering whether he'd been her mother's lover.

"I once thought my mother was having an affair with him," Samantha says. "This was when I was twelve or thirteen, when I'd just learned what an affair was. My parents were arguing a lot, and I was suspicious."

"How do you know she wasn't?" Danielle asks. She thinks to apologize for the bluntness of her question, but Samantha doesn't seem bothered.

"I asked her, years later, when I was having my little marital problems." Samantha sighs. "She couldn't even remember who Joe Greicius was." She pauses, shakes her head. "Or she pretended she couldn't." She shrugs. "Mothers. Who knows."

"Right," Danielle says. "Who knows."

The scoreboard clock over the south side of the rink shows five minutes left in the lesson. Alice leads her students in stretching exercises against the far wall. Natalie stands on the left end, and Danielle notices her glancing back out at the ice. *She'd rather be skating*, Danielle thinks. *Flying down the ice. This could be her passion, the way it was mine.*

She tries to imagine the life she would have lived if she'd continued skating, how she might have replicated off the ice the satisfaction and fulfillment she felt on it. She has trouble conjuring particulars, but instead finds herself full of longing, as if for something near but unreachable. When Natalie breaks free from the wall and flies down the ice, Danielle hears laughter and assumes it's her daughter's. But it's Alice's, the timbre bittersweetly familiar. Alice skates after Natalie and catches her hand. Gazing across the dream-white ice, Danielle imagines the two skaters are herself and her mother—that her mother, thrilled by their contact and their easy duet, is alive again with laughter.

BLACK TV

Robert Williams was, secretly, a fan of television—secretly because his wife, Sarah, the principal at Sherman Middle School, thought television was an abomination of the brain. For his wife, bliss was books and Broadway. (He and Sarah made a quarterly pilgrimage from Ohio to New York City to watch plays, musicals, and, once, a show so bizarre even "experimental" wasn't an accurate category.) So when the Sherman Ice Arena acquired a TV, Robert was—secretly—thrilled.

The new TV, which was mammoth and stood in the corner of the lobby, to the left of the gas fireplace, had been bequeathed by a wealthy former ice dancer. In his thirty-seven years as rink manager, Robert had never had a TV in his lobby. He'd had Pac-Man, Ms. Pac-Man, Defender, Centipede, several pinball machines, including a Who Shot J.R.? model, and, currently, both a Deer Hunter and Duck Hunter game. At one point in the mid-1990s, the lobby had hosted a ping-pong table, but its contests had spawned too many brawls between hockey players, so it had been retired to the shed behind the rink.

He loved the TV because he loved sitcoms and dramas and even soap operas. During down times at the rink, the TV made him feel less lonely. Indeed, it was so large he sometimes felt the actors were standing in the room with him. Moreover, it provided a means, if only virtually, to double or triple or quadruple the Sherman Ice Arena's black population, which generally included only him. Robert had a favorite channel, a channel he watched almost exclusively, a channel the white patrons of the rink, which is to say 99 percent of the rink's patrons, referred to, sometimes under their breath, sometimes with the boisterousness of Bull Connor on a bullhorn, as "the black channel."

Robert's first act as caretaker of the television had been to ban hockey players from the lobby. This may have seemed like a draconian measure. But as they waited their turn on the ice, hockey players could not be trusted to sit quietly or even avail themselves, for the relatively cheap price of a dollar, of the pleasure of the Deer and Duck Hunter games. Inevitably, they found a tennis ball or a stale donut or anything fist-sized and solid and employed it as a hockey puck, which they slapped around the lobby with a vigor they often failed to exhibit in games. Robert had a vision of a puck-substitute shattering his TV.

Naturally, the hockey players complained about their banishment. But Robert pointed out that they had a locker room in which to do whatever they pleased. "Turn it into a boxing ring," he told the grumblers. "Or bring in a couch and a coffee maker. Make it cheerful and homey, homey." (He smiled when he repeated the last word. He agreed with his wife: as a noun, "homey" was ridiculous.)

Weekend public skating sessions presented another problem. Immediately before and after each session, the lobby filled to capacity. Robert was worried that a child or a careless adult, in putting on or removing a skate, might jam a blade into the screen. In order to deter the public-skating crowds from going near the television, he decorated it with garlic, whose smell he amplified by slicing open every clove, and played reruns (the TV came with a DVR) of PBS fund-raising drives. The public, he was satisfied to see, gave the TV a wide berth, although he did field a complaint about the "devilish smell." (To this patron, he said, "At least it'll keep the vampires away.")

Robert could count on the rink's figure skaters to do the TV no damage. Alice Maravicious, the skating director, tolerated no misbehavior on the ice much less in the lobby. She'd once disciplined one of her skaters for merely impersonating a hockey player. (During a rehearsal of *Cinderella on Ice*, the skater had pretended to check the evil stepmother into the boards.) As they sat on the wooden benches and laced up their Edeas and Jacksons and Riedells, the figure skaters—there were twelve of them who showed up regularly for freestyle hours—gazed without malicious intent at the screen.

This didn't mean they liked what they saw.

He shouldn't have been surprised. But he'd hoped that because he knew these young women (and one young man), because he'd talked to them about the competitions in Cleveland and Columbus they'd competed in (but had rarely medaled in because, they claimed, the judges favored the home-town skaters), because he'd counseled them about life priorities when their time on the ice surpassed their time with their textbooks and they were in danger of failing algebra or biology or AP World History, because he'd even played matchmaker by introducing a pair of figure-skating sisters to a pair of ice-hockey-goalie brothers...because of all this, he expected the figure skaters to at least give the shows he loved a chance.

Fat chance.

One week was typical.

On Monday, Doris Pope brought her daughter, Rachel, in for her lesson with Alice. Rachel, who was ten, pointed to the television and said,

"There are even black people in the commercials!" and turned from it as from a rancid smell. (By this point, Robert had removed the garlic.)

On Tuesday, Tasha and Helen, the college-aged sisters whom Robert had introduced to the hockey goalies, sat in front of the TV as they laced up their bunny-white Edeas. Said Tasha: "You could play a drinking game with this channel. A shot every time a white person appears."

Said Helen: "Yeah, but you'd never get drunk!"

They both laughed.

On Wednesday, Mikaela Holmes, a junior in high school, attempted to change the channel manually. She ended up turning off the TV. Doubtless worried about being caught (she was the only person in the lobby), she fled to the ladies' room, where she remained for the next forty-five minutes.

On Thursday, Ella and Paulina, high-school-aged best friends, stuffed quarters into the Deer and Duck Hunter video games and lifted their respective rifles. "Look what Robert's stupid TV has made us do," Paulina whispered. "It freaks me out to kill even video deer, but I'm soooo bored."

On Friday, Frankie Farmer, a sophomore in high school who claimed to be a hockey player, but could often be found practicing lutzes and sit spins during power plays, did stand-up comedy for the other eight skaters in the lobby. By their laughter, they clearly preferred Frankie's fart jokes to whatever the TV offered.

Robert observed all of this on the black-and-white security screen in his office, located behind the floor-to-ceiling shelf of rental skates. The footage could have been an art-house documentary on racial insensitivity. But he didn't want to think of his skaters as racially insensitive. He liked his skaters—he thought of them as his, like a basketball coach might his players—and he was convinced they could, if they only allowed themselves to, see beyond their surface unease—black people everywhere!—and find in the shows he loved precisely and delightfully what he loved.

Surely, they would see in *Tavon's Afterlife*, a drama about a former football star who, after suffering a career-ending injury, becomes an inner-city high-school teacher, the beauty and courage of a man who loses his lifelong dream, but discovers a meaningful life.

And would they be able to resist laughing at *Brother, Brother, Brother*, a sitcom about a trio of brothers who share a Los Angeles apartment and pursue various careers—actor, restaurant owner, nurse—and the same sexy and smart woman?

And even if *The Cool of the Evening*, a soap opera set in Atlanta, was, to him, a guilty pleasure—all the men looked and spoke like Sidney Poitier (to whom Robert's wife, especially when romantically inclined, sometimes compared him); all the women were either beautiful angels or even more beautiful devils—it couldn't have been any less appealing than *The Young and the Lustful* or *The Days of Our Libidos* or whatever the white soap operas were called.

But what could he do? Force his skaters to watch and laugh and nod in delightful understanding?

One Monday, as he was again propped in front of his security screen (he had become, he was alarmed to discover, mildly depressed, preferring the quiet of his Peeping-Tom office to his usual social spot at the rink's front counter), the entire Sherman Figure Skating Club gathered in the lobby. Its members were meeting to discuss the spring show, a mash-up of fairytales from around the world. The show had been Alice's idea, and there would be, Robert knew from his eavesdropping, resistance due to the show's "weird," "foreign" and, preposterously, but predictably paranoid, "anti-Christian" storylines. The first complaint Alice heard when she stepped into the lobby, however, wasn't about her show.

Because the room was full, Robert couldn't tell who spoke. It might as well have been the entire crowd: "Could we please—*please*—find a channel that isn't all black people, all the time?" There followed a slight retraction: "I'm not racist, but..." followed by mumbles of agreement and soft imperatives to return white people to the screen.

Alice had been a regular at the Sherman Ice Arena since she learned to walk. As her parents' marriage crumbled, and as Alice's mother plummeted into depression, Alice found even greater refuge in the rink. She became an extraordinary figure skater, which is how she acquired her nickname—Alice Marvelous.

When Alice was thirteen, her mother committed suicide. In the aftermath, Robert and his wife had her over frequently to their house. They had attended dozens of Alice's figure-skating competitions. They had been in the audience at the U.S. Figure Skating Championships in the Staples Center in Los Angeles on January 13, 2002, when Alice had come within a missed triple axel of winning the title. He had once heard Alice, in conversation with a parent of one of her students, refer to him and Sarah as her "second, and better, family."

Nevertheless, Robert expected Alice, who was perhaps the most conciliatory person he knew, to say to her skaters, "Okay, okay, I understand. I'll talk to Robert about it. We'll find a compromise."

Instead, she exploded.

"Do you have any idea what it's like to grow up black and be surrounded by everything white?" she said. "Any idea what it's like to go to elementary school and read story after story about little white boys and little white girls? Any idea what it's like to turn on the television and see white face after white face and when you finally see a black face, it belongs to a drug dealer or a pimp or someone about to hold up a school bus full of kindergarteners? Any idea what it's like to live in a town where if people don't know you—and even if they do—they look at you like you might steal their car or rape their sister?"

Alice's black hair and pale skin made her the perfect Snow White (she'd played the part in two Sherman Figure Skating Club shows), but as she stood in front of the cowered skaters, she reminded Robert of Cleopatra or Joan of Arc.

"Listen," she said, "I know *The Cool of the Evening* isn't exactly high art. Good God, how many times has Lateesha Wright been married? Twelve? You'd think the writers would come up with a different plotline. How about giving the woman a career, for God's sake? And *Tavon's Afterlife* is a little too preachy for my tastes. The man is a saint. And having him save the entire school from that automatic-rifle-bearing psycho—a demonic white supremacist, of course—was overkill."

Robert tried not to be offended by her criticism. As far as he was concerned, Lateesha Wright, who looked a little like his daughter, was forever, and rightfully, disappointed by her initially passionate but later too-predictable-to-be-anything-but-boring husbands. And *Tavon's Afterlife's* armed psycho episode was his favorite!

"But," Alice continued, "if you aren't howling with laughter two minutes into *Brother, Brother, Brother*, you have zero sense of humor."

Right you are, Robert thought.

"If you don't want to watch the TV," she said, gesturing toward the big screen, "bring a book. And give Robert a break." Alice turned toward the security camera, suspended from the wall above the Pepsi machine. "I bet he's watching right now." She smiled and waved. "How'd I do, Robert?"

What followed over subsequent days and weeks was a movie an earnest white liberal director might have filmed.

The figure skaters did what Robert hoped they would do: They gave black TV a chance. And although *Tavon's Afterlife* never caught on with anyone but Frankie Farmer, who related to a macho athlete finding his softer side, and *Brother, Brother, Brother's* humor was hit or miss (one had to be black to understand it all, he supposed), the skaters loved *The Cool of the Evening*. Rather than complaining about the omnipresence of black characters, they were, after a couple of shows, debating about which of her three suitors Lateesha Wright ought to marry—or whether she should give up once and for all on happily ever after.

But of course the good times couldn't last. Upon returning from his latest Broadway trip—thumbs up to *Rats: The Cats Parody*, thumbs down to the actual *Cats*—Robert discovered a shattered TV.

Alice, crestfallen, explained: the skaters had been watching the "Lucky Thirteen" episode of *The Cool of the Evening*, in which Lateesha marries her baker's-dozen husband, when Frankie Farmer, probably in jest, called Lateesha a "whore." One of the skaters (Alice refused to say who but promised that the young woman would pay for the damages) was so outraged with Frankie's comment that she picked up a puck left behind by a hockey player and hurled it at Frankie. Her aim, Alice was sad to report, was "way, way, way off."

Whoever the culpable skater was never stepped forward to admit guilt much less buy a new TV. Robert never expected her to. One thing he and the figure skaters had in common was that they could not afford a $1999 television set. The rink's insurance company, meanwhile, dawdled and delayed. Eventually, the rink's owner preferred to settle in cash.

For weeks, the broken TV stood in the lobby. In the end, Robert and Frankie Farmer hauled it to the storage shed, where it sat beside the ping-pong table to stand as a piece of Sherman Ice Arena history.

Although Robert's wife noticed his down mood, he couldn't tell her about the TV. To do so, he would have had to explain his relationship with it, and she would not have approved. But Alice understood. Sometimes at evening's end, they stood together in the lobby, looking at the empty corner, wondering if, at last, Lateesha Wright was happy.

The fat girl was getting married. She was marrying a soldier who would be shipping out for Afghanistan in five days. She'd known him in high school, but they hadn't dated until the summer after their senior year. It was autumn now.

We weren't sure why she was marrying him. No, this wasn't true. We suspected she was marrying him because he was the best man she would ever catch. It was his motives we were unsure of. We'd never seen him, although he'd supposedly picked her up a couple of times at the Sherman Ice Arena, where we all skated after school. Our little group called itself the Future Olympians, but even at twelve and thirteen and fourteen, we knew we weren't talented enough to compete beyond regional competitions in Cleveland and Columbus.

This didn't stop us from judging other skaters severely. We ranked the fat girl low on the list. It wasn't because she was a terrible skater—she was better than we were, if we were to be honest—but because she sometimes practiced in baggy sweaters and because her skates looked as beaten up as rentals and, of course, because she was fat.

Her name was Vicky, although one of us had nicknamed her Vicious. She wasn't vicious, but she could be cranky. One afternoon, finished with our private lessons and restless, we were skating in frenetic pursuit of Frankie Farmer—who was a hockey player, but because his father gave money to the rink, he was allowed to share the figure skaters' ice time—when two of us bowled into her, knocking her to the ice. Before we could apologize, she snapped, "Grow up. This isn't a playground." We skated off sheepishly, but by the time we reached the other end of the rink, we were laughing.

She was a child herself although we didn't know it then. For the youngest of us, anyway, high school seemed remote and graduating from high school seemed like the other side of the moon. And to be married? Mars.

Vicky and her Afghanistan-bound boyfriend were married a day before he left the country. From the rink, only Alice Maravicious, whom we called Alice Marvelous, attended the wedding. She was Vicky's skating coach. She was our skating coach too.

Vicky didn't skate for the reasons we did. She didn't aspire to be an Olympic star or even to perform in one of the Sherman Ice Arena's biannual shows, the audience composed of parents, grandparents, boyfriends, and bored siblings. She skated because she wanted to lose weight. Weeks after Vicky's husband left the country, some of us overheard her mention this to Alice. We were in the bathroom of the women's locker room while Vicky and Alice were lacing up their skates in the dressing room. Alice had chided Vicky about failing to practice her footwork, especially her inside edges, and Vicky, with a sigh, had admitted that becoming an excellent skater wasn't what she hoped to gain from her time on the ice.

Skating, she told Alice, was the only sport she could do without embarrassing herself. She could run maybe a hundred yards, she said, before her knees ached and her lungs burned and she had to quit. In the swimming pool, she said, she floated rather than swam, which she could do just as easily in a bathtub. And on a bicycle, she felt like an elephant doing a circus trick. Besides, her butt became sore in seconds.

"But with skating," she told Alice, "well, it's not like I'm flying, but it's like—if I could only go a little faster—I could."

"Could fly like a blimp, maybe," Betsy Pound whispered. It was a miracle Vicky and Alice didn't hear our laughter.

We knew why the war in Afghanistan had started. But after a while, we didn't know why it was still going on. In truth, we didn't pay much attention to it. It was less invasive than the background music at the rink. We couldn't imagine Vicky's life—how she must dread a knock on her door—so we didn't.

Georgia, one of the Prodigies (which is what we called the figure skaters who were younger than we were), announced one afternoon in the locker room, "It's stupid to marry a soldier. He might die." No one who might have been offended by Georgia's remark was around, so we felt free to laugh. It *was* funny. Here was a nine-year-old redhead with pigtails speaking righteously about something she knew nothing about, yet we recognized a truth in what she said.

Our fathers weren't soldiers; they never had been. They were businessmen and lawyers and accountants and doctors. They wouldn't be foolish enough to sign up to die. They had us in their lives, after all. They needed to be around in case we needed them. We needed them when we needed them. The rest of the time we preferred to think we didn't have parents.

We didn't know Vicky's husband's name. Or we'd forgotten it. During the wedding, Alice had taken a picture of him and Vicky on her iPhone. One day, maybe because she heard us talking about him, she showed us the photo. He was shorter than Vicky, and with his round face and his big blue eyes, he didn't look like a soldier. He looked like a kid you'd see playing basketball by himself on the playground.

What did Vicky see in him? What did he see in her? Did he like fat skaters? Was Vicky a good cook, a good kisser? Maybe they liked the same music. Maybe they'd been lonely and they'd found they were less lonely when they were together. Maybe Vicky's husband was worried about dying, and he felt better knowing someone cared whether he died.

We didn't think much about them. We thought about our own weight, our own kissing (if we were kissing anyone, which mostly we weren't), our own music. We were lonely sometimes, but we had cures. Music was one. Movies. Long talks on the phone with our friends. No matter how bad we felt at any particular time, we knew our futures were bright. We weren't going to marry soldiers. And if we did, they wouldn't look like lonely basketball players. They would be as handsome as actors, and whatever they did in war, they wouldn't die.

Vicky's husband didn't die. But he was coming home from the war much sooner than he was supposed to. He wasn't injured. At least his body wasn't injured. But something was off with his mind. How did we know this? Alice didn't tell us. Perhaps our parents knew and spoke about it in front of us the way they sometimes did about their friends who were kissing people they weren't married to, as if they'd forgotten we weren't babies anymore, as if they'd forgotten we could understand. Maybe we overheard Vicky and Alice speaking in the locker room again.

When she discovered her husband was coming home, Vicky skated with special animation, whipping around the rink as if she were, in fact, flying. Maybe nothing was wrong with him, we thought. Maybe he'd faked being disturbed because he wanted to come home, and she was glad to have him back even if he'd lied. Maybe she was happy he wasn't coming home with one of his arms blown off or his butt full of bullets or, as Lizzie Garnett (who was fifteen and had let two boys touch her breasts, although on separate occasions) said, "Maybe she's tickled to death he hasn't lost what's between his legs." Maybe she was just happy he wasn't coming home dead.

She came to the rink again three days after he returned. She skated as if she were on air. Her legs seemed barely to move, yet she soared across the rink. She even smiled at us, although with a certain indulgence, as if we were ugly but innocuous dogs. Her happiness gave us permission to laugh at her again. We bestowed on her a new nickname, courtesy of the Spanish that Marcia Latrell was studying in middle school: Vicky Vaca. Vicky the Cow.

But the next time we saw her, a week later, her skating was distracted, plodding. She didn't notice us. We buzzed around her like bees, and she didn't so much as curse us under her breath. We could have knocked her over, and she probably wouldn't have said a word.

Thereafter, she came to the rink sporadically, and she often didn't stay long. One day, after she skated twice around the rink and left as if she'd run miles, Alice raced after her, not even bothering to put on her skate guards. From the ice, we saw them in the lobby, standing in front of the Ms. Pac Man game. Alice, who was in her mid-twenties, but seemed timeless, like the Good Witch of the North, spoke animatedly, occasionally reaching to touch Vicky's shoulder or grab her hand.

When we were older, we would look back at Alice with amazement. She was the only decent skating instructor in town, she ran programs designed to teach autistic and disabled children to skate, and on her days off she volunteered in the pediatric ward of the Ohio Eastern University Hospital. She remembered our birthdays and not only which schools we attended, but our classes and teachers. She knew our favorite songs. She knew how to be kind to fat skaters with troubled husbands.

When Vicky left the lobby, Alice, having unlaced her skates and put on her black tennis shoes, left with her. It was an hour before she returned.

As Alice stepped back onto the ice, her face looked like nothing we'd ever seen. She hadn't been crying; it was worse. She looked both sad and frightened. She tried to smile. She tried to smile the rest of the afternoon. She never succeeded.

Later, we wished we had shown Vicky a kindness or at least had said more than "hello" to her (if we'd even said this much). But we thought we weren't like her. And we weren't, but mostly, it turned out, because we were younger than she was and she had taken an express train to sadness. By and by, we would arrive at the same destination.

Lizzie Garnett swore she heard the shot. Her father was a divorce lawyer and her mother was an accountant and they lived in The Summit, Sherman's most exclusive neighborhood. But from her back deck, she claimed she could see, across an expanse of forest, the First Ward neighborhood where Vicky lived with her husband in a two-bedroom wood house painted army green. Lizzie had been standing on her back deck, gazing over the trees. "At first I thought it was a car backfiring or a dog barking," Lizzie said. "But there was such a stillness afterwards, you know? It was like I knew even when I didn't know."

A few months later, the Sherman Figure Skating Club held a fundraiser for Vicky. She relied on food stamps to eat. She couldn't meet the mortgage on her shoebox house. She wanted to go to college, so she could get a better job than working behind the counter at the Arctic Oasis in downtown Sherman. A local DJ, M.M. "Mad" Murphy, promoted the event on his 6 to 10 a.m. broadcast every day for two weeks. But on the day of the fundraiser, which we called "Great Skate for a Warrior's Widow," the spring weather was temperate and inviting, and even Mad Murphy didn't show up. The crowd was composed of the usual collection of family and friends. Sixteen skaters performed ninety-second solos except Alice, who performed a pair of three-and-a-half minute programs and landed a double axel in each.

Vicky appeared at the beginning of the event. She walked down a green carpet to center ice and accepted a bouquet of yellow roses from Alice. But although everyone expected her to stay for the entire show— she had been outfitted with a special suite, the visitors' hockey bench enhanced with cushions and soft drinks—she disappeared. Alice skated the opening and closing numbers. In between, we had our turns. We were told to pick solemn music, although our iPods had never hosted anything more sober than Pink's "Funhouse." Frankie Farmer, who was a part-time goth (he dressed in black three days a week), encouraged us to skate a group number to "The End" by the Doors. But it was a thirteen-minute song about a psychopath, and we couldn't agree on whether to perform camel spins or spirals during the part about children going insane. Lizzie Garnett was set to skate to a Nirvana song until the final rehearsal when Alice decided a performance to help the wife of a suicide might seem macabre if it featured music by a suicide. In the end, Alice steered us to the usual suspects in classical music.

We never learned how much money "Great Skate" raised, but it couldn't have been more than $300, including profits from the four skating lessons Alice raffled off.

Afterwards, in the locker room and, later, over dinner at Pizza Paradise, we merely noted Vicky's early departure from the show before we spoke about how well (or not-so-well) we had performed. Alice came to dinner late and didn't stay long. We left at dusk. If the sky was a mournful gray, we didn't notice.

Of course, when we grew older, we saw the great sadness in what Vicky had lived through and developed empathy and sympathy (we never learned the difference between them, but surely we possessed both) around what she'd suffered. Of course, we blushed at our teenage indifference and our inability to see beyond the borders of our little egos. Of course, of course.

But one afternoon, eight years after Vicky's husband killed himself, when a few of the Future Olympians were in graduate school and the rest of us were finishing college, we reunited the Saturday after Thanksgiving in Chelsea Bennett's house. Her parents were on a cruise in Mexico, so we behaved like the teenagers we'd been and drank too much beer and smoked too much pot. Frankie Farmer, who was in his junior year at Boston College, thanks to a hockey scholarship, suggested we go to the Arctic Oasis for ice cream. It was close enough to Chelsea's house to walk, and the night was temperate enough to make ice cream desirable.

The Arctic Oasis was located next to the Hope Theater, which used to show art-house movies, but had closed down a few months before. On its other side was a parking lot, which tonight hosted no cars. Set in the middle of darkness, and with its inviting pink and yellow sign, the Arctic Oasis did look like an oasis.

We stepped into the store, enveloped in cool air and the smell of chocolate syrup. The wall to our right was covered with school children's drawings, in crayon and colored pencils, of the Arctic Oasis's icon, a rainbow polar bear. On our left was a giant dispenser filled with red, white, blue, green, orange, and purple sprinkles. In front of us, behind a long freezer counter, stood Vicky. She looked older, which to us meant worse. She was heavier. Her face was paler. She had pimples on her chin and forehead. Her tag said Manager, but she was the only employee in the store. Perhaps whoever was supposed to work the shift had called in sick.

If she recognized us, she didn't say so. We had changed, of course. We had grown up. We had grown breasts or, in Frankie's case, a goatee. We looked more like our parents than we did our childhood selves.

It was up to us to remember her, to acknowledge her, and, if we felt inclined—and shouldn't we have?—to tell her what we never had. We could have said we were sorry about what had happened to her husband and what she had endured. We could have said, *We hope you're doing all right.* We might even have said, *And the goddamn war hasn't even ended,* and shaken our heads and asked her if she was still skating.

The eight of us exchanged glances. Any one of us could have initiated a conversation. Perhaps we were all waiting for someone else to start. But Lizzie Garnett said, "Well, I'll have a scoop of raspberry supreme with a teaspoon—no more than a teaspoon—of chocolate syrup. In a cup. To eat here."

And, one by one, we ordered our ice cream.

We pulled two tables together near the front window, sat down, and ate and talked about things so important we wouldn't remember them the next day.

From time to time, we giggled.

If we had glanced Vicky's way, we might have seen her standing against the back wall, tears sliding down her cheeks. Or we might have seen her wiping the silver counter with a blue rag, her vigorous strokes fueled by rage. Or we might have seen her writing an elegy on a receipt a customer had failed to collect.

We might have seen her gazing at us with pity, marking the distance between who we were and who we ought to be.

PROFILES IN PARANOIA

The new boy was a problem.

Philip (he didn't want to be called Phil) had moved to town only a month before, but already he'd become friends with everyone at the Sherman Ice Arena, from Robert Williams, the manager, to Eva Longstreet, who, at age six, was the Sherman Figure Skating Club's youngest member. A twelve-year-old, Philip had mastered all his single jumps and was working on his doubles.

Philip's sense of style was as memorable as his skating. As thin as a hockey stick, he liked to dress in uniform colors. One day, he wore black skating pants, a black T-shirt, and dark-tinted sunglasses. Another day he wore red skating pants, a red T-shirt, and a red beret. On a third day he dressed all in yellow, including a yellow scarf. The rink's skating director and chief coach, Alice Maravicious, whom everyone called Alice Marvelous, joked that Philip aspired to be every crayon in Crayola's 152-piece set.

Jim Agnew, whose son was also twelve and a figure skater, had concluded that Philip was gay. Even if Philip was a better skater than Charlie, and even if Philip's face and hair suggested a young John F. Kennedy, Charlie would, if only by default, be more successful with girls, which seemed to Jim the better battle to win. Although Charlie had expressed only a mild interest in girls, Jim's wife, Patty, insisted he'd had a couple of crushes.

Jim was a Professor of Political Science at Ohio Eastern University. His specialty was Richard Nixon. He was writing a book about politicians who, like Nixon, had damaged and even destroyed their careers because of personal animosity toward, or vendettas against, their real or perceived rivals. The book would open with Alexander Hamilton and Aaron Burr and would conclude with the 2012 Republican presidential candidates, who despised each other more than they despised Barack Obama. The title of the book, after John F. Kennedy's Pulitzer-Prize-winning study of politicians' courage, would be *Profiles in Paranoia*.

Jim was forty-six-years-old, and his health was excellent, thanks to a vegetables-and-whole-grains diet. After a period in which he wondered if his marriage, like an automobile left too long in the elements, would never run the way it used to, he and Patty had restarted their romance.

Jim couldn't say his life was perfect, however. His 1,200-page biography of Nixon, a volume he hoped would earn him a big award, had been greeted on its publication two years before with a kind of exasperation. "Do we need another Nixon book?" asked the *Columbus Dispatch*.

No, his life wasn't perfect, but it was as close to perfect as it would likely ever be. Or it had been, anyway, before his son's mood, once carefree, had slid into bitterness and quiet fury. Several times, Jim asked his son what was troubling him, but Charlie refused to say. Patty, meanwhile, chalked up Charlie's darker attitude to his age. "Puberty is as much an illness as it is a life stage," she said. "Unfortunately, the only medicine is time."

But one night, as Jim labored late on his book, he heard Charlie crying in his bedroom. His first thought was to wake Patty so she could intervene. Instead, he tapped on Charlie's door, whispered his son's name, and entered. "What's wrong, buddy?" he asked, dropping beside Charlie on the bed.

"Nothing."

"I don't think you're crying over nothing."

"Nothing important."

"If you're crying, it must be important."

Silence followed. At last, Charlie said, "I hate Philip."

Jim asked his son why, and Charlie's said, "He's better than me. And everyone loves him. Especially Alice. She loves him and hates me."

Jim was sure Alice didn't hate Charlie. Alice seemed incapable of hating anyone. If she weren't a figure-skating instructor, she would make a great life coach.

"Everyone loves Philip," Charlie asserted. "They love how he skates. They love the clothes he wears. They love everything he says."

Jim thought: He won't be so popular when all the girls who have crushes on him realize he'll never have a crush on them. But Jim didn't think this argument would move Charlie. So he said, "Alice likes you very much, Charlie. Of course she does. So does everyone else at the rink."

"But he's better than I am." Charlie listed what Philip could do on the ice, including his recent mastery of a double salchow.

"So work harder," Jim said. "It's good to have a rival. It will improve your game—your skating, I mean."

If healthy rivalries existed in politics, they were rare. John Adams and Thomas Jefferson became friendly and fabled correspondents only after their careers were over. During their political primes, they wanted to kill each other. Jimmy Carter and Gerald Ford wrote op-ed pieces together, but only after both men were out of office. Richard Nixon never met a potential rival he didn't detest. He was the Darth Vader of politics.

"It's good to have a rival," Jim repeated. "In the end, you'll thank him."

Jim and Patty alternated driving Charlie to and from the rink. When Jim was next on duty, he observed Alice as she coached Philip. With her black hair, red lips, and cream-colored skin, Alice looked like Snow White. But she would never have been fooled by a poisoned apple proffered by a jealous stepmother in disguise.

As she and Philip huddled, Jim focused on her face. Was it possible Charlie was right? Was she especially bright and animated around Crayola Boy? (Today Philip was wearing an all-green outfit, which made him look like an asparagus spear.) Although Jim suspected she was offering a correction to his double loop, he wondered if, given her smiles, they might instead be trading jokes.

Half an hour later, during Charlie's lesson, Alice smiled on a few occasions, but not as frequently as she had with Philip. And Jim noted this point: When she'd worked with Philip, she'd worn only a sweater with her skating pants. But before her lesson with Charlie, she'd put on her Russian overcoat. Thus covered up, she was, Jim concluded, holding in her warmth—and therefore withholding it from Charlie.

Jim recalled his conversation with Alice the previous week, when, after Charlie's lesson, they'd somehow found themselves discussing Richard Nixon. Jim mentioned to her, perhaps, he realized now, for the second or third time, that the *Dallas Morning News* had called his biography of the thirty-seventh president "illuminating." He always felt compelled to cite the Texas paper's praise in case whomever he was speaking with Google-ed his book and discovered all the (lamentably plentiful) mediocre reviews. He wondered now if Alice found his self-congratulations laughable. He wondered, furthermore, if she had projected her negative feelings about him onto Charlie.

But he caught himself, wise to the irony. He was being paranoid. He was being—Christ—Richard Nixon.

But not entirely. Because the next time Jim was at the rink, he again watched both boys' lessons, but this time with a scientific intention. On a pad of yellow legal paper, he tabulated the number of times Alice smiled during each lesson. During Philip's lesson, the total was eighty-two. During Charlie's? Twelve.

After Charlie's lesson, Alice strolled off the ice and spoke to Jim with her usual enthusiasm. Charlie had mastered both his inside and outside edges, she said. But he needed more power in his power pulls. "He seems a little frustrated," she said.

Jim was tempted to respond: He's frustrated with the favoritism you show other students, one in particular. Instead, he said, "He'll have it all down soon."

"I'm sure," she said, smiling. Was there irony in her smile, a knife-like implication that she was sure of the opposite?

Jim glanced at Philip at center ice. His music was playing, a classical piece Jim had heard before, but couldn't name. *Shouldn't he be skating to Frankie Goes to Hollywood?* Jim wondered. He caught himself. He was, he feared, again on the edge of homophobia, although he doubted anyone at the rink would have heard of the eighties band or its gay-themed hit song.

He recalled Nixon's quote about how homosexuality "destroyed the Greeks." In his Nixon bio, Jim had devoted several pages to exploring—inconclusively—the contributions of homosexuality to the decline and fall of the world's first democracy. Jim's "too obvious respect for Nixon's crackpot claims," said an *American Scholar* reviewer, gave his biography an air of "indiscriminate admiration."

On the ride home, Charlie sat morosely in the backseat. Jim thought he should again give him a pep talk about hard work and dedication, about focusing on what was in his control and what wasn't. But he also believed in being honest with his son. So he said, "I think you have a point about Philip." Charlie perked up, and Jim shared his survey results.

"I knew it!" Charlie said. "And did you see what he did...or what he didn't...today? He didn't even say hello to me."

He's an arrogant little prick, Jim wanted to say.

"He should be skating to Frankie Goes to Hollywood."

Jim *did* say that.

"Who's Frankie Goes to Hollywood?"

"Music from my generation. Frou-frou music."

"He likes Tchaikovsky," Charlie said.

"Who was gay," Jim said automatically, as if they were playing a word-association game.

Charlie didn't follow up on the subject. "He's working on his program for the spring show," Charlie said. "It's really good."

"Yours is good too," Jim said. He'd encouraged Charlie to skate to "Start Me Up" or "Born to Run," music Jim used to play in the car for both of his children. He considered listening to the Rolling Stones and Bruce Springsteen an essential part of their educations. Charlie had politely declined his suggestions, however. Instead, he chose music by Frank Ocean, a singer Jim had never heard of.

"I wish he would stop coming to the rink all the time," Charlie said. "There's no way I'll get better than him if he's always skating."

"Doesn't he have other interests?" Jim asked. "Maybe…I don't know…ballet?"

"He's like me," Charlie said, biting his lip. "He only wants to skate."

Jim recalled, as he often did, the recent—or relatively recent (to him, it felt like yesterday)—*New York Review of Books'* analysis of a dozen Nixon books published within the past couple of years. The writer, whom Jim used to respect, had discussed the books in order, as she put it, of their "worthiness." His Nixon biography had been in the penultimate spot, besting only a memoir by a former Nixon staffer. Jim had read all the other books and couldn't see how anyone could judge them superior to his. Furious one night, he'd written the critic a letter, heavy on biting counterargument (her choice as the top Nixon biography, he said, contained six errors in the first chapter alone!) and sarcastic threat ("I'll be sure to get a restraining order on your keyboard the next time I publish a book"). Predictably, he'd heard nothing in response.

"You're a better athlete than Philip," Jim told his son. "You're built like a man-in-training, not like a…" What word did he intend for the end of his sentence? Nothing kind. He sighed. "If you keep working hard, you'll be better than Crayola Boy."

His voice didn't convey conviction. Perhaps Charlie picked up on this because he said, "I doubt it."

The next time Jim was at the rink, his poll of Alice's smiles yielded roughly the same results as before. He did consider including in his data what might be described as a half-smile. Charlie seemed to earn more half smiles than Philip, but Jim ultimately discounted them, as they might be said to fall into a disputable category, like the hanging chads of the 2000 presidential election.

In addition to keeping score on Alice's smiles, he noted the responses of the six other skaters present, all young women between the ages of ten and eighteen. Though this survey was less scientific, as he couldn't observe every skater at once, it was obvious, by their words as well as their expressions, that they preferred Philip over Charlie by a wide margin.

Jim wanted to hurl his legal pad aside, step into the rink's open doorway, and shout, "What's wrong with Charlie? He's a good kid. Maybe he's a little morose sometimes, but he's solid and smart and…and, goddamn it, he isn't gay!" Once again, he felt appalled at himself. Was this, in the end, the best argument he had in his son's favor? And what kind of argument was it, anyway?

For the next hour, both Charlie and Philip worked on their programs for the spring show, silently alternating plugging their iPods into the rink's PA system. Philip, who had dressed all in rose, demonstrated a stage performer's panache, whipping around the ice and shooting his arms up and around as if conducting a wild orchestra. In contrast, Charlie approached his jumps and spins as if following a paint-by-numbers pattern. "He's a grinder," Jim said aloud, which might have been a compliment in another sport—football, for example—but sounded damning when applied to figure skating.

So his son wasn't a natural. So what? Plenty of people succeeded in their chosen fields despite lacking a natural aptitude. There was, for example…well, Nixon, of course. Jesus. Bad example. There was George H.W. Bush, whom, despite his one term, historians and political scientists now ranked right up there with Eisenhower and Wilson.

Alice hopped off the ice, grinning. "He makes me laugh," she said, probably to no one. But Jim followed up: "Who does?"

Alice turned to him, her eyes blinking as if to put him into focus. "Philip." She smiled. "I told him he should do stand-up, and he said he does—unintentionally—every time he tries to solve a problem at the board in math class."

You should see how funny Charlie can be, Jim wanted to say, although he couldn't remember having laughed at anything his son had said. Ever? Ever.

Alice smiled, slapped on her skate guards, and strode into the lobby.

Life is unfair. Not Nixon's quote, but Kennedy's. One boy is born with charm, dashing good looks, and deft comedic timing. Another boy is born with...doggedness. Oh, Christ, Jim thought, Charlie's only twelve years old. In a year he might be the most elegant figure skater in the state. Or he might be done with the sport, which would be fine with Jim.

But he suspected Charlie would stick with figure skating even as he slowly saw the gap between his accomplishments and Philip's expand. Jim had gone to grad school with a woman named Eileen Bloomstein, who never seemed serious about anything but marijuana. (*You know, it's a funny thing, every one of the bastards that are out for legalizing marijuana is Jewish.* Nixon again.) Yet Eileen was now a tenured professor at Cornell and the author of six books, including what *The New York Times* called "a surprisingly revelatory and appealingly irreverent" biography of the teenage Bill Clinton.

The next morning, a Saturday, Jim found Charlie in the kitchen, dressed in an all-orange outfit. "What's with the carrot costume?" Jim asked his son.

"Ha, ha," Charlie said with a frown. There was a pause. "Maybe it's his clothes."

"What do you mean?"

"Maybe everyone likes Philip because of his clothes."

Jim knew this couldn't be true, but he didn't contradict his son. The boy was approaching his rivalry with Philip in a scientific way, analyzing the data, testing hypotheses. Jim appreciated the effort. At the same time, there was something agonizing about it.

"I don't remember you having orange pants," Jim said.

"Mom and I bought them a few days ago."

As Jim drove Charlie to the rink, he thought about how his son's efforts to appear more like his rival would only make him look more ridiculous. He thought of politicians who had gone down a similar, ridicule-inviting road. In his second debate with George W. Bush, Al Gore had toned down his egg-headedness so as to seem like a regular guy. The result was a worse performance than his sigh-filled, exasperation-laden first debate effort. And of course there was Michael Dukakis, who, in an effort to appear as tough as his war-hero opponent, had driven an Army tank. With his oversized military helmet and cartoonish grin, he looked like a baby on a Big Wheel.

Sure enough, when Alice saw Charlie in the lobby of the Sherman Ice Arena, she asked, with a smile, if he'd intended to impersonate a traffic cone.

As Jim watched Alice instruct Philip, he again counted her smiles. His wrist quickly became tired. By contrast, Alice's lesson with Charlie might as well have taken place in a morgue.

With both lessons finished, Alice skated off the ice and gave Jim a quick rundown of what Charlie needed to work on. Jim didn't listen closely; he was thinking, Your allegiance is elsewhere. Charlie and Philip were now alone on the ice. Philip's mother—his father lived with his second family in California—had, as usual, dropped her son off and disappeared.

Jim saw Philip and Charlie confer at the announcer's booth. No doubt they were negotiating over whose music would play over the PA system first. Presently, Charlie smiled; it was such a rare sight Jim didn't trust he'd seen it, but he figured Charlie had won. What played wasn't music Jim recognized as Charlie's, however, and he felt a heaviness inside him. His son had been defeated again. *It is necessary for me to establish a winner image. Therefore, I have to beat somebody.* Nixon's critics cited this quote to emphasize his pettiness, but Jim understood it as only logical: winning depends as much on the competition's weakness as on one's own strength. Ronald Reagan became known as a warrior by beating up the impoverished island of Grenada, after all.

Philip swept around the ice like a speed skater. Perhaps, Jim thought with reluctant admiration, the boy could have been a hockey player. What brutish defenseman could keep up with him?

Jim glanced at Charlie, who touched his throat, his signal that he was thirsty. Jim had forgotten to bring in his son's water bottle from the car. He didn't feel like walking to the parking lot, so he grabbed change from his pocket and stepped into the lobby. The vending machine was in the corner.

When he returned, bottle in hand, he stepped into the open doorway to the ice. There was a six-inch step down to the surface, and he tapped his shoe against it. Charlie, at the far end of the rink, saw his father, but instead of hurrying toward him swirled into a slow spin. Philip approached from Jim's left, inches from the boards, speed-skating in his all-purple outfit like Barney after Weight Watchers. Philip was fifty feet from him...forty-five feet...forty. Jim anticipated feeling a rush of cold, stinging wind as Philip passed him.

Thirty feet, twenty-five.

When had Charlie last been happy? When, for that matter, had he? Christ, he couldn't stand the taste of defeat, the way he felt like hanging his head all the time.

Fifteen feet, ten feet.

When Philip was no more than five feet from him, Jim stuck out his foot. He braced for the impact of the boy's shins against his ankle. He rehearsed surprise, an apology, words of concern. But Philip's reflexes were extraordinary. He leaped like he was jumping a creek, clearing Jim's outstretched foot and landing as gracefully as if the interaction had been choreographed.

In the immediate aftermath, Jim wondered if he had only fantasized his intention to trip Philip. But the next moment, the boy turned, a quick, decisive twist of his head. Even as his momentum carried him toward the end of the rink, he gave Jim a look both stunned and full of disgust. Their eyes locked, and as much as, afterwards, Jim wanted to imagine the boy didn't understand his intention, he knew otherwise. For months, Philip's expression would haunt him, prickling his happy moments, reinforcing his darker moods, shaming him like nothing else in his life.

Presently, Charlie approached, his leisurely, almost lackadaisical, skating a contrast to Philip's speed. When he reached his father, he made a quick stop, doubtless intending to spray him playfully with ice, though he raised only a few shards. Charlie's smile was ebullient, stretching his face in such a way as to make him seem, with his orange outfit and flat square teeth, like a gleeful Jack-o-Lantern. For a moment, Jim thought Charlie had seen what he'd tried to do and had come to thank him for his contribution, however unsuccessful, to the war against Philip.

"Guess what?" Charlie said, beaming. "Philip asked me to do a duet with him in the spring show. We're gonna skate to the theme from *Star Wars* and carry light sabers. Isn't that cool, Dad?"

TORNADO

She appears in my dreams as a tornado. The settings vary. A dusty plain. The downtown of a major metropolis. My backyard. Although I never see her face, I know who she is. I feel the wind in my hair. I feel the danger and thrill of her nearness. I feel so close to death I know I am alive. And always when I wake up I am disturbed by how still the air is.

I've seen Alice Maravicious—Alice Marvelous is her nickname—do scratch spins, lay-back spins, Biellman spins—the figure-skating equivalent of tornados—at the end of Learn-to-Skate sessions, for which I signed up my daughter, having failed to interest her in bowling and basketball. Alice's spins are designed to show the young skaters she instructs what they, too, could do one day. During the actual lessons, Alice and her assistants skate between four- and six- and eight-year-olds, preventing them—and sometimes failing to prevent them—from falling. Some of the children fall so often Alice allows them to use walkers like old people would. They shuffle around the ice like miniature residents of a retirement home.

At Learn-to-Skate, Alice doesn't wear the sleek, glittering dress she used in competitions. (Photos of her on-ice triumphs, including a fourth-place finish in the U.S. Nationals, decorate the lobby of the Sherman Ice Arena.) She wears a Russian overcoat, like Julie Christie in *Dr. Zhivago*. She could be in Red Square in winter. Often I imagine myself meeting her in a world apart from the heavy world I inhabit. She is twenty-five years old, and I have more gray in my hair than black. I am old enough to be—I hate to consider the math and hope my calculations are off—her father. But in these worlds I envision, I am ageless.

I am married to my second wife. Ten years of wedded bliss. Or less-than-bliss-but-better-than-loneliness. Or better-than-I-deserve. Or come-to-think-of-it-downright-good-maybe-even-great. We have a beautiful daughter and a beautiful house. Even our dogs, a pair of golden retrievers who might have stepped out of a hunting calendar, are beautiful. My wife and I both have good jobs. We have good friends. We buy good wine and watch good movies and have good, albeit infrequent, sex.

I cannot be having a mid-life crisis. I had my mid-life crises toward the end of my first marriage, manifested in a new car, a new career, and—the marriage killer—a new woman. I am supposed to have arrived at serenity. At Learn-to-Skate sessions, I should be checking my email and index funds. I should be gabbing to other parents about football and 401Ks and climate change. Hell, I should be comfortable and contented enough, as I sit under the warm air tumbling from the box heaters above the bleachers, to, every so often, close my eyes and drift into tornado-free sleep.

I am not supposed to sit like a rapt pilgrim at a holy shrine, studying Alice's movements as if each spin were a hieroglyph or a piece of scripture.

Sometimes I wonder if my dreams are about heaven. Alice's swirling presence might suggest the obliteration of my sins and the chance, in the beyond, for a clean slate and a glorious afterlife. Sometimes, however, I worry my dreams represent my incapacity, my impotence. She is the life force I no longer have—and now fear in others.

I used to see a psychologist. But in his absence—he and I parted ways after I remarried, when I thought my dark days were over—I share my dreams only with good people gone from my life who live on in my head: my third-grade teacher, who assigned me the seat in front of her desk and shared her lunch with me; my uncle Joe, who drank too much but listened to whatever I told him; my first girlfriend, whom I dumped because I was young and stupid. Sometimes they tell me my dreams have no meaning but are only the random videos the YouTube of my mind plays. Sometimes they joke with me, say *The Wizard of Oz* must have stamped itself on my subconscious. Sometimes, most times, they simply smile at me, as if they haven't heard what I've told them or as if they, too, don't understand—or understand and don't wish to share what they know.

Sometimes I imagine telling Alice about my dreams. I imagine her revealing she has the same dreams, except in them she is swirling around a still point. "You," she says in this happy fantasy, "are the still point." In her dreams, I am what cannot be moved, the counterpoint to her tornado, as strong in my stillness as she is in her whirlwind. "Yin and yang," she says. "Thesis and antithesis. The unstoppable force and the immovable object."

To the real Alice, I say little beyond, "My daughter's learning a lot from you." And: "She isn't falling down half as much as she used to." And (joking): "A few more weeks and she'll be ready for the Olympics."

Do I want Alice to fall in love with me? Do I want to sleep with her? Of course not. Of course not.

Of course. Of course.

But more—or less—I don't know—I want her to explain her presence in my dreams. No, to assure me my dreams are good omens. No, to sweep away my loneliness and leave me satisfied with my own company. No, I want...

Perhaps the tornado is my confusion.

The days disappear.

At the end of the penultimate Learn-to-Skate session, fortified only by the drinks I've imagined myself drinking, I decide to tell Alice about my dreams. I will make fun of them. I will say, "Maybe I'm obsessed with major weather events. Tonight I'll probably find myself in a flood." I know—of course I know—that there is something strange and inappropriate about what I am about to tell her. But if I don't tell her, I might never stop dreaming of her.

Maybe I am hoping she will reveal to me something I could never have suspected.

When the last Learn-to-Skate student steps off the ice, Alice follows. I catch her in the near corner of the rink. I stutter, lie, tell her I want to discuss my daughter's progress. (My daughter, meanwhile, has slipped into the lobby to warm her hands by the gas fire.) My words tangle, collide—they swirl like the tornadoes I've dreamed of. Alice waits, a patient smile on her face.

A moment passes. Alice looks at me questioningly, as if for permission to excuse herself. Now I tell her—do I? do I actually say this?— I tell her I love her. But I don't mean it in the way she thinks I mean it. I mean it in the way one might say "help" when one isn't in any immediate danger, but feels the presence of something foreboding approaching on the horizon, or in the way one might say "Lightning" and not be referring to what blazes across a thunderous sky, but to a horse one dreamed of owning in childhood. Black save a white zigzag across its forehead, a horse capable of bearing its rider past every danger.

Or perhaps I mean it as a surrender, an acknowledgment of language's inability to describe what I don't understand. Perhaps "I hate you" would have been equally as inaccurate. But, no: "I love you."

"I'm glad you love what I've taught your daughter," Alice replies. Has she misunderstood what I've said? No, she is offering me a passage back to respectability. There is such grace in her gesture, I bow. She blinks twice, as if to dismiss the entire scene, and slips into the lobby. For a long time, I stand in the cold rink, listening to the hockey players who have stormed the ice like soldiers into a vulnerable city.

The final Learn-to-Skate session will culminate in a show dubbed "A Festival on Ice." All of the Learn-to-Skate students, including twin six-year-old boys who wear hockey helmets and like to smash each other against the boards, are to perform brief routines to their favorite songs. The Learn-to-Skate instructors, Alice's four teenage assistants, are to perform as well. So, too, is Alice.

The Festival on Ice is to be held three weeks before Christmas, two weeks before Hanukah, some time before or after Kwanza and Ramadan and Diwali. Alice asks the four fathers who regularly bring their daughters to lessons—"the gentlemen," she calls us, perhaps because she doesn't remember our names—if on the night of the festival we will string holiday lights around the rink. She asks the mothers if they will run the bake sale. One mother balks, deciding on her role: bouncer.

The day of the festival is bone cold, its skies filled with full gray clouds. Working with the efficiency of an elite bridge-blowing unit, the three other fathers and I hang our lights in thirty-seven minutes.

My wife joins me a minute before the show starts. She explains her tardiness: a meeting at work, bad traffic…etc…etc… This is the third time in the past two weeks she has shown up at the last minute to an event. I might be suspicious and suspect an affair. I might even desire such a scenario; it would serve as an easy explanation for my unease. But I know my wife isn't having an affair. She simply works too hard; she always has. I must search elsewhere for the source of my disquiet.

The first twenty-nine routines preceding Alice's are filler, white noise, droning previews. In my mind, I cross out each performance as it occurs, even my daughter's. I am counting down to Alice's performance. Twelve skaters to go…eight…six…three.

When the oldest of Alice's assistants leaves the ice after her program, the lights dim and a hush falls over the arena. Or perhaps the hush is in my heart. In the window at the far end of the rink, snowflakes light up in the darkness like white fireflies. Alice skates to the center of the ice and holds a pose. The lights slowly come up, showing her in a white blouse and black poodle skirt, her hair in a pair of ponytails. She has put twin suns of rouge on her cheeks and her nose is red from the cold. Her white skates seem disproportionally large on her feet. If I were capable of thinking it, I might think she looks like a clown.

No, I am the clown: a man who is too old to be so adrift, so baffled by life. Disgusted, I excuse myself. "Bathroom?" my wife asks. I nod as Alice's music—not "Send in the Clowns," but something playful and light, like a breeze or a whistle—begins.

I don't need the bathroom, but I go anyway. I stare into the mirror above the rust-stained sink. I see a middle-age man who thinks his dream of a tornado is some kind of portent or promise. But it's only the swirling dust of his mind.

I return to the rink, stand alone against the Plexiglas at the far end as Alice finishes her program. As she curls into her final spin, the flag below the scoreboard shudders, snaps. The Plexiglas trembles, threatens to shatter. From the crowd come cries of astonishment and awe. I close my eyes. The entire building shakes. My dream, I realize with satisfaction, but also with fear, was prophecy. Some kind of end of days is upon us. But when I open my eyes, the rink is still, the applause diminishing to silence. I have imagined everything. The crowd files into the night.

Minutes later, my wife finds me. "Coming?" she asks.

I remind her about my duty to the lights.

"Right," she says.

With the same efficiency as before, the three others fathers and I remove the lights from around the rink. My fellow fathers are, I realize from their banter, good friends. As our task concludes, they mention grabbing a beer at Don's Underground and ask if I would like to join them. I decline, tell them I'll finish up our job. I watch them march out of the arena and into the snow-filled night. I stow the boxes of lights in the giant cupboard at the west end of rink. After I lock the cupboard, I gaze out at the empty ice.

I've failed to understand something. Or I've failed to realize there is nothing to understand. I laugh like someone pretending to laugh.

I step outside into snow. The falling flakes are as large as hands. In the distance, at the end of the parking lot, I see a woman in a black coat crouched beside her car. The snow in her hair makes her seem ancient, a witch, a crone, but I hear her softly crying like a child. I plow toward her; there must be half a foot of snow on the ground. When I am within a few feet of her, she looks up.

"I've lost my keys," Alice Marvelous says, sniffling and swiping her ungloved hand across her nose.

As if a curtain has been opened in front of me, I see her not as a mystical life force, a tornado capable of sweeping aside all my problems and bearing me up and over my limitations and into a land of rebirth more glorious than Oz—no, I see her as everything she has been and is and will be, from an infant to a beautiful figure skater and a kind teacher to a white-haired woman. Perceiving her like this, I see myself in a similar way, as someone who, although living in a middle-aged body, carries everything I've once been and am and will be within me—in my soul, in my psyche, in my memories and presentiments, even in my body—and I realize, in the kind of epiphany too obvious to celebrate, that I am the tornado, that we all are, everything past and present and future whirling in one concentrated force, mortal but freer from time than we think as we move across life's landscape.

Like the good father—the good son (Alice's snow-white hair makes me feel youthful by comparison)—I was and am, I kneel in the snow and stick my bare hand under her car's left rear tire. It isn't long before I touch her keys. After standing, I hand them to her without ceremony. She throws her arms around me, a quick embrace, perhaps a pardon for my words of the week before. "Thank you, thank you!"

She thanks me again before she opens her car door, slips in, starts the engine. She waves as she drives off.

I should feel blessed or absolved. I should, at least, feel relieved to be at the end of a mystery. But even as I pull in a deep, satisfied breath, the snow swirls around me, clouding my eyes. I wave my hands but nothing comes clear.

GOODBYE, GOODBYES

<u>First Panel</u>
An older girl spins at center ice; a younger girl skates cautiously near the boards, her arms extended for balance. The older girl, who is fourteen, wears tights, a short pleated skirt, and a T-shirt with "Skate USA" written across the front. Tina, the cartoonist, isn't sure there is such an organization as Skate USA. There is, she knows, a Bowl USA. Her soon-to-be-ex-husband used to bowl every Tuesday at lanes owned by Bowl USA. She erases "Skate USA" and pencils in "Winter Olympics." But will her readers think the older girl is an Olympic skater? She is supposed to be a good skater, no more. What Tina wants to convey is that the older girl is entrenched in the local skating world. The younger girl isn't—at least not yet.

Tina erases "Winter Olympics" and writes "Sherman Figure Skating Club." But this is too long a name. In newspapers—twelve still publish her strip, *Main Street Madness*—the words would be too small to read. She erases them and writes "Sherman FSC." She outfits the younger girl, who is eleven, in a heavy winter coat and gloves. She wants to include finer details: the older girl wearing her own (expensive) pair of figure skates; the younger girl wearing rental skates. She suggests this in the condition of the skates, the older girl's sleek and new, the younger's old and worn.

If Tina were to be honest—and who wants to be honest when honesty scares?—she would concede that her comic strip is dying. With the mass extinction of newspapers, she may soon be drawing *Main Street Madness* exclusively for her hometown paper, the *Sherman Advocate and Post*, which, seemingly alone among its black-and-white-and-not-read-all-over contemporaries, has held on to a steady readership and advertising base.

A couple of years before, Tina decided to seek a larger audience by writing a graphic novel. The endeavor proved more challenging than she expected. Used to producing economical, four-panel strips (eight panels on Sundays), she struggled to summon multiple characters and complex plotlines. Several months passed before she drafted a first chapter. She was often in a dark mood, and this saddened and frightened her daughter, who was ten, and annoyed her husband, who had agreed to assume a greater portion of the childcare and household responsibilities as she worked on her novel. Her husband became more annoyed when, after reading the first three chapters of *Goodbye, Goodbyes*, he saw himself in the character of the failed painter who becomes a bartender.

It was true that her husband had failed to realize his dream of becoming a musician. But there was a difference, she insisted, between a bartender (the character she'd created) and a bar owner (her husband). "You think I'm a failure," her husband accused half a dozen times over the next few weeks. In retrospect, she thought there was something exaggerated in his wounded demeanor, as if he were looking to find a cause he might blame for the disruption he'd already planned. One night, tired of defending herself against his grievances, she said, "You're a middle-of-the-road guitarist, a so-so singer, and the owner of the fourth best bar in a ten-bar town. Life goes the fuck on."

She apologized immediately, but she knew she'd said something irrevocable.

Second Panel

The older skater and the younger skater, who have become friends, spin side-by-side at center ice, smiles on their faces. Tina intends the smiles to convey more than joy. They express (she hopes) the radiant feeling of finding a kindred spirit, someone who celebrates the same moments and music, someone who understands without explanation. Both skaters are now wearing "Sherman FSC" T-shirts. They wear identical skirts. The younger skater no longer wears rentals, but brand-new figure skates.

Because it is a public figure skating session, other skaters appear in the background. One of the skaters occupies a prominent spot to the left of the young women. He is a boy the older skater's age and wears a T-shirt that says "Tigers," which is meant to suggest his predatory nature. He is as handsome as she can draw him, with wavy black hair and inviting dark eyes. His eyes—she hopes this is obvious—gaze greedily, hungrily, at the older skater. Neither the older skater nor the younger skater notice him. They are enamored with skating, with what their agile bodies can do, with their blooming friendship.

If she were to be honest—that dreadful phrase again—she would admit that today's cartoon is about her daughter. In the last three years, Ella, now twelve years old, has grown from a novice skater into a dedicated athlete who skates five times a week. Twenty months ago, she joined the Sherman Figure Skating Club, where she at first was the shy girl at the end of the rink practicing her waltz jumps and spirals in anonymity. But she was a quick study, and her skating improved so fast that even her coach, whom everyone calls Alice Marvelous, said, "I would be surprised if she isn't landing all of her doubles by the time she turns fifteen." She didn't become friends with the girls her age in the club. Rather, she and a more advanced skater named Paulina, three years older than Ella, became best buddies. When Tina mentioned to Alice how sweet, but unexpected, she found this relationship—no older girl Tina knew when she was her daughter's age would have befriended her—Alice said such relationships weren't uncommon in the figure-skating world. "Girls of the same age and skill level become rivals," she explained. "Girls of different ages and skill levels support each other."

Ella and Paulina spent hours together off the ice, although skating infused all their conversations. They filmed videos of themselves performing off-ice axels, lutzes, and toe loops. They followed well-known skaters on Instagram and attended a "Stars on Ice" performance in Cleveland. They watched YouTube videos of figure-skating bloopers, howling with laughter.

Third Panel

The handsome young man, now wearing a "Lions" sweater, stands beside the older skater, who has stopped skating in order to speak with him. To her other side, her young friend performs a sit spin. The older skater, who, like her friend, wears a "Stars on Ice" T-shirt, Is clearly flattered by the young man's attention, clearly enamored of his wavy hair and winsome face. The smile she wears is intended to say: *I'm curious about the world you're inviting me to join.*

The limitations of four and eight panels, and a desire to tell a longer story about love, in several manifestations (between spouses, between siblings, between friends), were why Tina had wanted to write a graphic novel. To devote herself to *Goodbye, Goodbyes*, she put *Main Street Madness* on hiatus, the way Gary Trudeau had done years before with *Doonesbury*. Although she continued to work three days a week as an art teacher at the Tree of Knowledge, a private elementary school, the loss of the income she earned from her comic strip meant that she, her husband, and Ella had to watch their spending. One of the casualties was her daughter's figure-skating lessons, which dropped from three times a week to once a week. Ella said she understood. But Tina overheard her, on the phone with Paulina, say, "I'll never land my axel now. And forget my double salchow. "

Her husband's displeasure with the character supposedly modeled on him made it difficult for her to work on her novel. Their estrangement grew. He appeared occasionally at meals, less frequently in her bed, often choosing to spend the night on the couch in the den. She thought to speak to a friend about the unnerving degeneration of her marriage, but cocooned in what used to be the blissful life of her family and more recently obsessed with the writing and drawing of her novel, she had allowed her friendships to atrophy. She'd twice permitted her two closest friends' birthdays to slip past unacknowledged.

When she rewrote her book to make the husband's character an investment banker who, because he works fourteen-hour days, is largely absent from the story, her husband balked.

"I see," he told her. "I'm invisible."

"You're working, providing for your family," she assured him, abandoning, because she was tired of fighting him on the point, her insistence that the husband's character wasn't modeled on him.

"I think you'd like me to become invisible," he said.

"No," she said. "I think it's you who want to disappear."

The conversation had taken place in the living room. In its aftermath, to her horror, Tina had found Ella in the adjacent foyer, practicing camel spins on a shoe-sized spinner Paulina had given her for Christmas. She might not have heard them. She might have been pretending she hadn't heard them.

But other, even more fraught, conversations followed. Tina tried to reassure her daughter about what was happening, but she sometimes failed to fill her words with conviction. Ella, however, didn't seem phased. Whatever her parents' troubles, she still had skating; she still had Paulina.

Fourth Panel
Is her cartoon about her daughter or herself?

She would like to think she is aiming at a universal experience, something all women have felt in their lives, the pull between romance and friendship. (Men, she supposes, face a similar conflict. John Lennon chose Yoko Ono over the Beatles, after all.) Carly, the woman her soon-to-be-ex-husband is now dating, used to be her friend. Tina and her husband met her at a party thrown by the *Sherman Advocate and Post's* publisher. Ten minutes into their conversation, Carly told them, in detail spurred no doubt by the wine she'd drunk, about the end of her marriage, an event so recent, Carly said, she had RSVP'd to the party on behalf of both herself and her husband.

Feeling sorry for Carly, Tina invited her over for dinner on several occasions. Twice, she also invited over a single male friend, so the meal would be *a cuatro*, but nothing clicked between them. Tina could assume later, however, that things had clicked between Carly and her husband, though he insisted they'd become lovers only after he'd decamped to an apartment in Partytown, Sherman's college-student-dominated neighborhood.

She hasn't seen Carly in months, although a week ago Carly sent her a card, saying she hoped they could remain cordial "for Ella's sake."

The humiliation of having a friend jump into her husband's bed would have stung less if her graphic novel had sold. But she couldn't even find an agent to represent it. She must have tried forty agents; the last wrote back to say he found the book's ending, in which the protagonist resurrects her deceased friend by drawing a cartoon of her that comes magically to life, "as sentimental as it is implausible."

Meanwhile, when she was ready to return to *Main Street Madness*, six newspapers told her they were dropping her strip. Three had folded. The combined circulation of the newspapers for which she now draws is 278,522 (Sundays) and 212,654 (weekdays). A quarter of a million potential readers are more of an audience than most artists enjoy. But at the height of its success, *Main Street Madness* reached more than four million readers.

She will be okay; Ella will be okay. Okay was, of course, never her dream. She will draw *Main Street Madness* until the last newspaper drops it or folds. She will consent to the divorce her husband wants. He will probably marry Carly, and Tina will worry about Ella abandoning her for the stability and warmth of a two-parent home. It's possible Tina will remarry one day, but at the moment love feels like walking onto an iced-over lake during a thaw. She prefers the safety of shore.

She will be okay; Ella will be okay. But it pains Tina to finish today's strip because it isn't only about Paulina throwing Ella over for a high-school hockey player with shoulders as straight as a soldier's and a go-ahead-and-hate-me-because-I'm-beautiful smile. When Paulina disappeared abruptly from Ella's life, Ella cried for three straight nights. Nothing—not even her promise to bring Ella to the U.S. Figure Skating Championships in Boston the following year—soothed her. On the third night, sitting next to Ella on her bed, exhausted and worried about the depth of her daughter's pain, Tina herself cried, which proved the antidote to Ella's tears, her daughter's sadness replaced by alarm. "What's wrong, Mom?" she repeated until Tina's "nothing" sounded sincere enough.

No, today's strip isn't only about Ella and Paulina. It's also about her and her older sister, Marilyn.

When they were growing up, Marilyn, whose eyes were as bright and blue as Tina's were smoky and dark, employed her sister in her "Great Dramas," as Marilyn called them until she was old enough to be embarrassed by the hyperbole. They began when Marilyn was seven and Tina four, and consisted of simple, one-act living room performances. Marilyn was always the heroine, Tina always the sidekick. The villain was usually an off-stage presence, but was sometimes portrayed by Rascal, the family's Persian cat.

The girls' parents, noting their daughters' passion, signed them up for summer theater camps. As if the instructors had witnessed their homegrown productions, they always assigned Marilyn the lead and Tina the role of second banana, which, rather than disappointing her, thrilled her. In one early production, she played Toto to Marilyn's Dorothy and barked as if every line Dorothy spoke was a sunrise. One summer when Marilyn was fifteen and Tina twelve, they performed as Hamlet and Horatio in an unconventional (and abridged) version of the Shakespeare tragedy. The director, a college student with six earrings and a Mohawk, was so impressed by their chemistry he wanted to cast them as the leads in his stage adaptation of *Thelma and Louise*, although he'd yet to write it and never did.

During the run-up to performances, Marilyn and Tina rehearsed in Marilyn's bedroom, pausing occasionally to praise each other and critique their fellow performers' lackluster or inept efforts. After shows, they spent hours reviewing their performances line by line. They celebrated their certain futures as Broadway stars.

But at the end of the *Hamlet* summer, Marilyn met a high-school senior named Otto. He was tall, green-eyed, and wavy-haired. In contrast to the way Tina saw her sister, with religious admiration, he often seemed indifferent to Marilyn. To Tina's horror, this made Marilyn like him more. Marilyn spent an oppressive number of hours talking to him on the phone. She stopped acting because, she said, she wanted to "liberate my life" to be with Otto. She was smart and had excellent grades. She could have gone to a good college. But she decided to attend the mediocre university Otto attended in the southern part of the state.

One April day, after a three-and-a-half-hour bus ride, Tina walked unannounced into her sister's dorm room, her voice trembling with tears, and asked Marilyn, "What happened to us?" Calmly, in a manner Tina might have found patronizing if she could bring herself to criticize her sister, Marilyn said, "Just because we're sisters doesn't mean we have to be joined at the hip."

When Otto broke up with Marilyn in his senior year, Tina thought she might win her sister back. But within a month, she was dating someone else.

The man her sister eventually married isn't unkind. But first he moved Marilyn across the country. Then he moved her to Perth, Australia. Tina rarely sees Marilyn or her three children. Ella sometimes forgets she has cousins.

Tina's final panel shows the younger skater stalled at center-ice, her expression meant to suggest sadness, betrayal, and resignation. (Has Tina ever tried to draw so much emotion on a single face?) Behind her, the older girl is skating off with the wavy-haired young man, their faces turned toward each other, their hands linked.

Tina pulls her pen from her Bristol paper and regards her creation. "God damn," she mutters, not because she's gotten it wrong, but because she's gotten it—painfully, perfectly—right.

ICE RADIO

Alice Maravicious found the idea absurd. A radio broadcast of the United States Figure Skating Championships?

Was there a sport more dependent on the visual than figure skating? A fan needed to see the bold, the beautiful, and the (infrequently but memorably) bad dresses. The broad, pristine ice. The powerful spins. The elegant and athletic jumps. A fan needed to see the tension on skaters' faces as, huddled with their coaches in the kiss-and-cry box, they awaited their scores.

You had to be there. Or you at least had to see it on television.

But when Harold Abromowitz, a college classmate of her father's and the manager of WWHY in Cleveland, asked Alice if she would be the "play-by-play" announcer for the championships, she said yes. She said yes despite what the U.S. Figure Skating Championships represented to her: the most spectacular and most painful failure of her life.

She was, she supposed, bored. She'd been the skating director at the Sherman Ice Arena longer than she liked to acknowledge, and she knew the place like a mouse knows its running wheel. She knew she shouldn't think of her life as a cage; she was familiar with real human cages, having, several years before, visited her ex-boyfriend in a prison in Argentina. She also knew she shouldn't think of herself as a mouse; as she sped toward her thirtieth birthday, she was, as she'd been told by a pair of unsuitable suitors, more attractive than ever, the baby fat having disappeared from her cheeks, allowing her black hair to frame the ever-more-engaging angles of her face. Finally, she knew she shouldn't think of her career as a running wheel, forever going nowhere fast; in the past three years, she had doubled the number of skaters in the Learn-to-Skate program and tripled the number of shows produced each year by the Sherman Figure Skating Club. (This past season's lineup: "Holiday on Ice," "Snow White on Ice," and "Being and Nothingness on Ice," the latter a collaboration with the Ohio Eastern University philosophy department.)

Her latest, and most popular, project was "Adult Singles' Night" every Friday at eight. It featured local musicians playing covers of 1980s pop songs as well as free espresso shots and remaindered volumes of poetry, courtesy of the Book and Brew. Although Alice herself qualified as an adult single, she eschewed participation in her innovation, preferring to hunker down in her office against the earnest invitations of men who had grown as familiar and dull to her as her hometown.

If Harold Abromowitz had offered her money to drive a bus across the country or to track down rumors of witches in New England or to count polar bears in the Arctic, she probably would have said yes.

Ice radio?

Why the hell not?

As a twenty-year-old, Alice had been one of the country's best figure skaters. At that year's U.S. Championships, she was sure she would prove herself *the* best. Until the final night, until she returned to earth after executing her signature, celestial jump—a triple axel—she *was* the best.

But whatever her on-ice prowess, Alice didn't know anything about describing skating to an audience of radio listeners (if, indeed, anyone would actually be listening). Therefore, in the weeks preceding her on-air debut, she practiced by narrating her students' every move as they stumbled and flew across the Sherman Ice Arena's familiar surface. Skating, she realized, contained a lyrical vocabulary flush with alliteration and assonance: sit spin, scratch spin, double loop. At times during her broadcast rehearsals, she sounded like a slam poet.

Before long, she was in a booth in CheapLoans Arena, in downtown Cleveland, a microphone in front of her. Alice's partner, the "color commentator," was a Puerto Rican named Julio. She'd expected him to be gay. It was, of course, stereotypical to hear "male figure skater" and think, immediately, "gay." But the stereotype was ingrained in her nevertheless.

Julio wasn't gay. He wasn't even a figure skater. His single qualification for the job was that, as a doctoral candidate in anthropology at Case Western Reserve, he was writing a dissertation comparing traditional Puerto Rican dances as performed in Puerto Rico and New York City.

"Have you ever skated?" she asked him two minutes before their broadcast was set to begin.

"Does roller skating count?" he asked.

"Sure."

He thought about this. "Never," he said, and smiled.

Julio knew Harold Abromowitz because his niece was in a ballet class with Harold's granddaughter. "He figured figure skating and dance are the same discipline on different surfaces," Julio said. "I had my doubts, but I didn't want to ruin my radio career by saying so."

Julio had straight black hair and skin like cedar. He was half a foot taller than her five-foot, seven inches, and as thin as a hockey stick. He wore a tweed jacket, with squares of beige, black, and scarlet, and he wasn't shy about smiling. He had lovely teeth and his breath smelled like peppermint.

"I've never met anyone from Puerto Rico," Alice admitted forty-five seconds before their broadcast.

"I bet you've seen *West Side Story*," he said.

"The Jets versus the Sharks," she said. "'Tonight, tonight, won't be just any night.' Of course."

"I've never been in a gang," he said. "And I can't sing." He paused. Eighteen seconds left. "But I'm good with a knife."

"Seriously?"

"In the kitchen."

He smiled. White teeth and peppermint.

"Good evening, ladies and gentlemen and listeners across the planet—or at least across greater Cleveland—I'm Alice Maravicious and, with my broadcast partner, Julio 'Bon Appétit' Morales, I'd like to welcome you to the U.S. Figure Skating Championships."

Even at major figure-skating competitions and exhibitions, Alice was always surprised by how unimpressive most of the skaters were. It wasn't that they were bad or, really, anything less than excellent. And perhaps the pressure of performing in front of large audiences thwarted them from skating their best. But during the day's first event, the men's short program, she witnessed a dozen skaters stumble, skid, or fall. For her radio listeners, if they existed, she noted each failure with, she was aware, a kind of exasperation, as if to say, How could someone who has spent the last decade of his life skating six times a week, three hours a day, be so ordinary?

As a skater, she had been extraordinary....up until the end. In first place at the U.S. Championships after the ladies' short program, she was the final skater in the long program. In the middle of it (2:41 seconds into it, to be exact), she leaped into her triple axel. She soared, she spun—once, twice, thrice—and landed. She'd over-rotated by a couple of inches, but this wasn't her undoing. This was: She landed on the tip of her blade, spun like a racecar on black ice, and crashed onto her ass. She knew she should leap to her feet and resume, but she felt a heaviness descend on her. Seconds, which might as well have been centuries, passed. At last, she rose and skated a listless, out-of-rhythm conclusion. The applause was polite, the worst kind. She finished fourth.

During her broadcast, as she watched skaters cheat jumps or outright flub them, as she observed them spin less like electric drill bits and more like drunken tornadoes, she tried to infuse her play-by-play with compassionate explanations of how, after years of practice and thousands of dollars' worth of the best coaching in the country, failure was possible. But she still didn't quite understand her own failure, still thought it worthy of exasperated condemnation, and therefore couldn't be as generous toward the country's best skaters as they no doubt deserved.

"From my perspective," Julio said, "Tim Yang is skating his heart out. You can see the determination on his face. Or maybe he's fighting a migraine. In any case, I say, 'Bravo.'"

"Bravo," Alice repeated. She tried to add more enthusiasm: "Bravo!" However, she couldn't help amending, "But his triple toe loop looks like something he bought off the rack in the Jumps Department at J.C. Penney."

Julio glanced at her. Smiled. "Yes, there was a certain loose, cheap look to it. Next time, Tim, try Bloomingdale's."

It was a four-day competition, with the men skating on the first and third nights, the women on the second and fourth. Pairs skaters and ice dancers filled the rest of the bill. When the first night was over, Alice had narrated the shortcomings and triumphs of forty-eight skaters. Her mouth was dry. Her head throbbed. She'd run out of synonyms for everything from "ice" to "effort" to "better luck next year."

"You were tough," Julio said at they stepped out of the booth, "but brilliant."

"Brilliant?" she said doubtfully.

"Your descriptions...well...I bet if I'd closed my eyes, I could have pictured everything on the ice."

Her look remained skeptical.

"Or maybe everything you said was bullshit," he said. "What would I know?"

He offered to buy her a drink at the hotel where Harold Abromowitz had booked them rooms. The hotel turned out to be a bed-and-breakfast run by Harold's ex-wife, Gertrude, who had dyed, sunset-orange hair and wore earrings in the shape of compasses. She offered them bourbon. They drank it in the B&B's first-floor "library," which,

Gertrude explained unapologetically, had recently served as the bedroom of her now deceased father. Rather than books and bookshelves, it contained a hospital bed and a nightstand with a pyramid of prescription bottles. The room smelled of dried roses and something less savory. Alice and Julio sat side by side in armchairs across from the end of the bed.

Julio held up his glass. "To a new voice in radio," he said.

"To two new voices," Alice said.

They clicked glasses and drank. She couldn't remember the last time she'd had bourbon. Never was her best guess.

"If two new voices in radio have no audience," Julio said, "do they make a sound?"

"We should do an experiment tomorrow," Alice said. "Announce one of our cell phone numbers on air and say whoever calls in first wins free tickets to...I don't know...*West Side Story*."

"I wonder where it's playing."

"In at least fifty middle schools across the U.S.A."

They drank again.

"I have a confession," Julio said. "I did my research. I looked you up."

"'Alice Marvelous' was a nickname my mother gave me. I'm not Napoleon. I didn't crown myself." She realized she was speaking preemptively, and defensively, but often the first question anyone asked her was about her nickname.

A bemused smile danced at the edges of his mouth. "You don't like your nickname?"

"It isn't exactly fitting."

"You were a tremendous skater."

"In the biggest moment of my life, I fell short," she said. "Or, rather, I simply fell."

"On a triple axel," he said. "It wasn't like you flubbed a waltz jump."

"Look at you," she said in mock surprise, "with your skating terminology."

"I studied," he said. "A little." His smile softened, then disappeared. "I'm sure it was a huge disappointment. Devastating even." He touched his chin with his index finger. "If I don't have anything in my life to compare it to, it's only because I was never remotely as good at anything as you were at skating. But I've had my downfalls."

"Name one," she said, an edge in her voice.

"Case Western Reserve was my sixth choice of grad schools. My top five said no."

"Oh," she said, the edge gone. "Sorry."

"We can move on to happier subjects," he said, and drank.

Alice lifted the bourbon to her lips but put the glass down. "You read about my mother, I'm sure," she said. "You read about her suicide and how I'd dedicated my performance—in the long program, at the U.S. Championships—to her."

"I did," he said.

"It's one thing to screw up a jump," she said. "It's another to dedicate a program to your dead mother, have everyone in the building rooting for you because they feel sorry for you, and then..."

Jesus, Alice thought, *I refuse to cry*. She drank, chocked on her drink, and coughed. And coughed. And coughed again.

"You okay?" Julio asked.

"It was a decade ago," Alice said. "I've moved on."

She asked him about his dissertation. Five minutes into his explanation, he yawned. She followed. He yawned again. She did the same.

"It's late," she said.

"When I talk about my dissertation," he said, "it's late even at ten in the morning. I may be the only person alive with the talent to turn Puerto Rican dance into a sleeping pill. Fortunately, boring is a prerequisite for earning a doctorate. My advisor would be suspicious if she thought I was having fun."

It was after midnight, and they made their way to the second floor.

"Looks like we're rooming next to each other," Julio said.

"Great," she said. "You'll probably be able to hear everything I say in my sleep."

"Unfortunately," he said, "I think I'll be too tired to listen."

They said good night.

On the whole, the women at the U.S. Championships were better skaters than the men. But perhaps because she was a woman and had been in their boots, Alice was harder on them. She critiqued everything from their dresses (she used the word "garish" three times, "skimpy" twice, and "hmm" once) to their spirals and their double lutzes.

"I don't know if I would call Mary Kate Crawford's dress garish," Julio amended. "On the other hand, listeners, you might think of the color as what would happen if Christmas and Halloween had a child."

"Red, green, black, and orange," Alice said. "It's a holiday mash-up."

"But I love her enthusiasm, her energy, her…oops."

"No excuse. It's only an axel, a jump she's probably been landing since she was twelve."

At one point in the evening, a WWHY assistant sneaked into the booth to provide them with their dinner: turkey sandwiches and coffee. "What?" Julio whispered to Alice. "No bourbon?"

The evening's second half featured the eight best women's skaters in the country performing their short programs. Alice found herself drawn to Alexandra Maples, a nineteen-year-old from Muncie, Indiana. Alexandra, like Alice, skated in the Russian style, with big gestures and great athleticism but was, as Alice had been, a little unpolished. Alice decided Alexandra must be largely self-taught.

"I'm going to guess her formative years were a little like mine," Alice said. "She's a rink rat whose parents were absent or indifferent. She found coaches where she could, but, basically, she learned new moves and jumps from watching skating on TV or, in her case, the Internet."

"It says in her bio she's been training with Ivan Lev Lermontov since she was four," Julio said.

"*The* Ivan Lev Lermontov?" Alice asked.

"Or a rather bold identity thief."

"Ivan Lev Lermontov could turn the Three Stooges into gold medalists," Alice said. "If she doesn't win, she's Larry, Curly, and Moe's sister."

Julio glanced at Alice. Smiled. "No pressure, Alexandra," he said.

After the second night of the championships, they again delved into Gertrude's bourbon. To Alice, warmed by the liquor and Julio's gentle voice, the B&B's library now seemed less like an antechamber of the hereafter and more like a postmodern art exhibit.

"Tell me three things I should know about you that I don't know already," Julio said.

"I don't know everything you know about me," Alice said.

"I know you talk in your sleep."

"Did you hear me last night?"

"Loud and clear."

She was aghast. "What did I say?"

"'Why.'"

"Why? Because I'm curious, that's why."

"No. You said, 'Why.' Three times. Reminds me of the joke about the philosophy exam. 'Why?' was the single question on it. The only two passing answers were 'Why not?' and 'Because.'" He smiled and drank and smiled again. "Assume I'm familiar with every single entry about you on the Internet."

"Would it be a safe assumption?"

"God, I hope not. That would make me an extraordinarily thorough cyber-stalker rather than a slapdash one."

She drank her bourbon. "My father used to be an alcoholic."

Julio looked suspiciously at the glass in her hand.

"I'm not an alcoholic," she said. "At least, I wasn't before tonight." She had another sip. "But who knows."

"You said he used to be an alcoholic?"

"He quit drinking after my mother's suicide. He also quit womanizing, which was an odd time to quit, since he was suddenly single."

"And he's been sober ever since?"

"He fell off both wagons a few years ago. Delved into vodka and married women."

"A dangerous combination."

"Almost killed his career—he's an English professor. But he's good now. He drinks pomegranate juice. And he got remarried, to a fellow professor."

"Do you like her?"

"With a kind of lingering loyalty to my mother, I was prepared to hate her," she said. "But she's wonderful."

"So much for the evil stepmother."

"What about you?"

"I don't have much to say. You're more interesting."

"No, no, no," she said. "You don't get to be my broadcast partner, my drinking buddy, *and* my shrink. Tell me something about you."

"Did I tell you about my dissertation?" he asked, and laughed.

"Here's something crazy," he said.

"What?"

"After all this is over, I want to go skating."

"Consider it a date," Alice said.

As their broadcast began on the penultimate night of the championships, Alice glanced around the CheapLoans Arena and noticed a number of spectators wearing earphones. Although she knew it was likely to humiliate her, she said into her microphone, "Julio and I are curious this evening about who might be listening. If you're in the CheapLoans Arena and you're tuning in, would you please stand up?"

The arena was a quarter full, with perhaps 6000 people in the seats. After Alice spoke, at least 400 of them rose to their feet.

"Wow," Alice said with genuine surprise.

"Either they're listening to us," Julio said, "or everyone has to go to the bathroom at the same time."

"How about waving now?" Alice said.

Four hundred people waved.

"Oh, my," Alice said. She felt like she'd received an award and should somehow acknowledge it. "Thank you. You're very kind." She paused. "And now that I know you're out there and actually listening, I probably won't have a single insightful thing to say for the rest of my life." Presently, she fell silent, the radio broadcaster's equivalent of writer's block.

To fill the void, Julio spoke about the bomba as practiced in Mayagüez and Spanish Harlem. He started off promisingly, describing the dance's essential tension—sexual, seductive—between the drummer and the dancer, before drifting into a soporific discourse on the differences between the dance's basic rhythms: sica, yuba, cuembé, babú, belén, cunyá, leró, holandés.

Worried they would lose their audience as quickly as they'd gained it, Alice interrupted: "I'm looking for hard-luck stories tonight because, when I was a competitive skater, I was a hard-luck story. Or at least people told me I was. Yes, my mother killed herself when I was thirteen, but my father somehow sailed our ship well enough, so I could compete seven years later at this very event. Some of you know the ending: I fell and lost, but..." She didn't know where to go.

Julio rescued her: "Our first skater, Mauricio Caal, is definitely a hard-luck story. When he was six years old, he fled his native Guatemala and its civil war with his mother and sister and moved to Orono, Maine. His family rented an apartment literally right across the street from an ice rink. Thirteen years later, he's here competing to be the best male skater in the U.S.A."

"What a sweet story," Alice said.

"And there he goes—a sweet triple lutz."

"Actually, a double toe loop," Alice said. "But sweet indeed."

Back at their B&B, the bourbon continued to flow. "You couldn't drink it all up if you stayed until the fourth of July," said Gertrude, her compass earrings replaced by stars. "My boyfriend drives a truck for Jim Beam. Every other weekend, he brings me a bottle. I can't stand the stuff. With me, it's Pinot Noir or nothing."

Gertrude left them in the library.

"Maybe after all this is over," Alice said, lifting her glass, "we should head straight to AA."

"After this is all over," Julio said, "I don't think I'll touch bourbon again."

"No?"

Smiling, he gestured to the hospital bed and the pyramid of prescription bottles next to it. "I'll always associate it with painkillers and a faint smell of dirty Depends."

"I'll always associate it with you."

She'd meant her remark to be charming without being inviting. She wasn't successful: His smile threatened to overwhelm his face.

No, she thought. *I'm not doing this. This isn't something I want or need.* She didn't know if either of these assertions were true. What was true: She hadn't enjoyed a successful relationship since...well...high school. For her, the dating scene had been like a street-corner card game in which, shown the ace, you're supposed to pick it from three downturned cards. She'd never picked the ace. She'd picked plenty of fives, a couple of twos, and definitely one joker.

"We're here to work," she said, more forcefully than she'd intended.

His smile vanished. "Of course," he said.

"What I mean is..." She didn't know what she meant. She was a few weeks shy of her thirtieth birthday, and she wasn't sure of much beyond her newfound fondness for bourbon, which wasn't necessarily a good revelation. If she had discovered an affinity for Verdi operas or Japanese Noh plays, she might have had something to celebrate. She worried she was boozing her way back to a primitive and painful time in her life.

"Are you okay?" Julio asked.

"I don't know," she said. The liquor was affecting her in strange ways. Or perhaps in predictable ways. "Maybe I'm worried about seeing my mother's ghost."

"Sorry?"

"The ladies' free skate is tomorrow."

He looked at her quizzically, but also sympathetically.

"Do you want to hear a strange story?" she asked.

"Sure."

"After I fell at the U.S. Championships, I stayed on my ass far longer than I should have. Do you know why?"

"Shock, right? Didn't you tell me so? For Alice Marvelous to fall— it must have been unthinkable." There was kindness in his voice. Had she, a few seconds before, insulted him somehow? She hoped not. She liked him more than ever.

"I thought I heard my mother," she said. "No, let me be honest. I felt my mother on the ice with me. I felt her behind me—her hands on my shoulders."

"I'm sure," he said.

She was confused. "You're sure?"

"Metaphorically, you mean."

"Literally." She sighed. *He thinks I'm crazy. Maybe I am.* "I hadn't thought about her much in the previous...I don't know...five years. But here she was, standing behind me. She had long, beautiful fingers, but I never knew how strong they were until they gripped my shoulders and held me fast to the coldest ice I'd ever been on."

"Maybe she was hoping to help you up," Julio said uncertainly. "Metaphorically or...literally. You'd dedicated your performance to her."

"I never dedicated my performance to her. Some reporter had it in his head that that's what I'd told him. And once it was in print, it became the truth." She sighed. *Now he'll think I'm crazy* and *cruel.* "The truth was—the actual truth was—I'd tried desperately to forget her. So when I fell, I felt like—well, I thought, You deserve it."

"Deserve it?"

"For pretending to have dedicated my program to her when...honestly...I hadn't and never would have but maybe should have. And people had been cheering for me—crazily—because they thought I was such a sensitive, forgiving, generous daughter. But I was a fraud because even as they cheered, I thought, She's the worst kind of parent. A dead parent."

"She had an illness."

"A mental illness. And of course I understand how crippling depression can be, how life-threatening. I did then and I do more so now, especially as I've walked through a few of those terrible valleys myself. And I did, I did feel…"

"Feel what?"

"Guilty."

"For what?"

"For not saving her life? Maybe. I'll tell you *that* story some day, although it's probably no different than the story of any child of a suicide: 'If I'd only said this, if I'd only done that, if I'd only been a better child…'" She frowned and shook her head. "No, I think I mostly felt guilty for not being truthful with her—with her ghost, I mean, with her memory—and with everyone."

"What would being truthful have meant?"

"To have admitted I wanted to win for myself, for all the work I'd put in, for all my predawn hours at the rink, for all the parties I'd missed in high school because I was in a dinky hotel in Atlanta or Detroit, waiting to compete the next day. But…"

"But?"

"I thought it was so selfish to want happiness—to want success—when my mother had been so miserable, when she'd felt like such a failure. It was so selfish to want joy when she'd drowned in its opposite."

"No," he said. "I don't think so at all." He touched his chin, his contemplative gesture. "As a figure skater, you're alone on the ice, and if you want to perform your best, you can't be anything but self-contained, self-centered. What do athletes call it? 'Playing within yourself.' To even consider anyone or anything else is to risk grave distraction." He smiled. "A bomba—bear with me here—requires tension between the drummer and dancer. It doesn't succeed otherwise. But if you're on the ice and you hear a drumbeat—metaphorically, I mean—in the form of your mother or your father or your own guilt or doubt or whatever—you're suddenly confronting an additional tension beyond the immense pressure of performing."

"But it was so selfish of me to really, really, really want to let her go. Forever."

"No," he asserted, "it was essential. And not just for skating, but for living."

His gaze was somber. Hoping to brighten it, she offered him a grateful smile. "Well," she said, "why didn't you tell me this ten years ago?"

Alice wasn't crying, but Julio was.

"Did I say something wrong?" she said.

He wiped furiously at his eyes.

"Did you...did your mother...or someone you loved...commit...?" she asked.

"No," he said. "Not at all." He swiped at his eyes again. His tears shone like translucent jewels. "As you've discovered, I'm a little sentimental...I mean, stories such as yours..."

"Yeah?"

"You're an amazing woman who has suffered." He picked up his glass.

"Is that a toast?" she asked, lifting her glass.

"Why not?" he said, and they clicked glasses and laughed.

"Oh, Christ," she said.

"What?"

"You better tell me you're married or have a fiancée."

"Why?"

"Otherwise..."

"What?"

"Let's save it for tomorrow, after we've stopped being coworkers, colleagues, broadcast partners. It's the proper, professional thing to do."

"Of course," he said.

She leaned over her armchair and kissed him.

He smiled. "I thought you said..."

"I'm going to blame the bourbon," she said, and kissed him again, "even if it's blameless."

Was it selfish to love the U.S. Figure Skating Championships more for what happened off the ice than for what happened on the ice?

Alice wasn't thinking only of Julio, sensitive, sweet, and, on one subject, anyway, boring Julio. She was also thinking about the crowds who greeted them in front of their radio booth at CheapLoans arena before their final broadcast. The crowds wanted their autographs, wanted to have their pictures taken with them, wanted them to chat, via FaceTime, with their friends who were unable to find tickets to the sold-out ladies' long programs. Alice and Julio had become overnight (or over three nights) famous. And more fame was forthcoming: the following Monday, Alice would receive a call from a WWHY vice president inviting her to become the station's roving "life correspondent." The job: to offer commentary for half an hour three times a week on, in his words, "whatever the hell you want." There was also the possibility of a call-in show.

Alexandra Maples won the ladies' singles championship. To Alice's satisfaction, she didn't attempt a triple axel. No American woman had attempted a triple axel in a major competition since she and Tanya Harding had graced the ice. (Japanese women, on the other hand, were pushing toward a new frontier: a quadruple axel.) But no one at the U.S. Championships could match Alexandra's combination of athleticism and unflinching execution. She may not always have been elegant, but she never cheated a jump, much less fell on one, and her spins were exceptional in their controlled fury.

"Is there any advice you could offer this young skater?" Julio asked Alice as Alexandra, on the podium, leaned over to receive her gold medal. "Or is her life simply perfect now?"

"It was perfect the second she finished her program," Alice said. "She knew she'd won gold. Now, it's the Olympics. And after the Olympics, it's life, which never stays perfect for long. But you keep going." She whistled softly. "You keep going, Alexandra. And everyone else who competed here, and everyone who filled the seats tonight, and everyone listening—you keep going, too. If you're delivering letters, keep delivering them the best way they can be delivered, damn the pit bulls in your way. If you're teaching third-graders, keep bringing your A-game even if none of your students deserve A's. And if you find yourself sliding, slipping, falling—forgive yourself your failures, rise up, and keep going."

She laughed. "You have to keep going," she said. "Why? As the philosopher answered, 'Because.' Or, as a longer-winded philosopher said, 'Why not?'"

"Thank you, Alice."

"Julio, you're crying."

"Yes, Alice. Yes, I am."

"For my broadcast partner, Julio 'Waterworks' Morales, I am Alice 'Feeling a Little More Marvelous Now' Maravicious. Thank you for listening. Good night."

It was past midnight, and they had the CheapLoans ice to themselves. In fact, save a sextet of indulgent cleaning women who'd long ago finished sweeping up popcorn boxes and mopping up spilled ketchup—and were now standing against a rail on the mezzanine level—they had the whole arena to themselves. The trunk of Alice's car perpetually housed a pair of her figure skates; she'd asked Harold Abromowitz to find a pair of rentals for Julio.

Alice had attempted to teach Julio how to skate. He'd fallen three times. Now he fell again—without, it seemed, having moved a single muscle. "I should have yelled, 'Timber,'" he said. She offered him a hand. He grabbed it and squeezed it before letting go.

"Don't want help up?" she asked.

"I like my seat," he said from the ice. "Better than front row."

"Front row to what?"

"To your performance."

"What are you talking about?"

"I've been dying to see you skate." He smiled. "Let's see it," he said. "A triple axel."

She was about to say something, but didn't. "Okay," she said instead.

She skated twice around the rink, blazed toward the middle of the ice, and leaped into the air, spinning and spinning. She landed cleanly. She raised her arms in triumph.

Smiling, she skated over to him. He grinned like a peppermint-scented sunrise. "Amazing!" he said. "You did it!"

He read something on her face. "Wait," he said. "Was that really a triple axel?"

She smiled back at him. "Don't you know?"

"Of course not," he said. He held out his hand to her. She grasped it. But instead of her pulling him up, he pulled her down, onto the ice and into his arms.

It would never pass for a pairs' lift. But the six cleaning women on the mezzanine applauded their approval.

THE DRIVE

She had left the other girl, Aurora, back at the gas station. She hadn't planned it this way, but when Aurora said she needed to use the bathroom and May said she didn't, Lara knew what she had to do. She knew it as clearly as if it had been her design from the beginning. She pulled out of the gas station, an Exxon—there was something significant, she thought, about the double exes, like crosses—and back onto Route 45 to Akron. From the backseat, May, who was seven-and-a-half, said, "Wait! What about Aurora?"

Aurora, a blond with pigtails whose parents celebrated every spring equinox with a maypole dance, was twelve. Sometimes she sat in the back of Lara's car with May, sometimes she sat up front. It depended on how mature she wanted to seem. Today she had sat up with Lara, fiddling with Lara's iPod, playing one song, cutting it off, playing another. In the backseat, May had stared out the window.

The Sherman Ice Arena was closed—the refrigeration system had failed, which, because it was early June, had led quickly to mushy ice—so Lara was driving her two figure-skating students to the IcePalace in Akron. Rather, she had been driving both of them. When she pulled out of the Exxon without Aurora, and May had protested, Lara said, "She wasn't feeling well. She has her cell phone. She'll call her mom."

Now May says, "I didn't hear Aurora say she was sick. When did she say she was sick?"

"A minute ago," Lara says, "as she was walking to the bathroom."

"Shouldn't we wait until her mom comes?"

"She'll be fine. She's practically a grown up."

Lara expects May to argue, but there is silence in the backseat. In the rearview mirror, she sees May's hands covering her mouth as if to stop a scream. She wonders if she should have put May in the front seat. It would be more certain this way, she thinks. The two of them, together, quickly. She isn't, Lara sees, wearing a seatbelt. Lara isn't either. So it probably won't matter. A truck, head-on. To survive the impact would require an intervention from God.

Lara stopped believing in God—no, in love and life—when Jason Tanner, May's father, said they needed to stop seeing each other. The whole thing had been good fun, he said, and he cared about her deeply, truly, but—and this he had admitted sheepishly, like a boy confessing to stealing a cookie—he was getting married. Next month! It had been easy for him to hide this relationship; his fiancée lived in Sheridan, thirty miles west of Sherman. Even May hadn't known about her until recently.

Lara had imagined how she and Jason might tell May about *their* engagement. She imagined how thrilled May would be. What better stepmother than her skating coach. Lessons for free—any time she wanted! But when, as they skated a cool-down lap after May's lesson two weeks before, May told her about Bethany—Bethany, what an insipid name, Lara thinks—Lara felt terror flow through her as if she'd been told she had cancer. She didn't leave the ice in a rage, but in a stupor. As May unlaced her skates in the lobby, Lara motioned to Jason, who'd been watching the lesson from the bleachers. As they stood next to the Pepsi machine in the corner, she said, "May told me." She didn't need to say more.

"I was going to come clean," he said. "I was putting it off because I care so much about you. And also, I guess, because I'm a coward."

His smile was warm and contrite. He was the handsomest man she'd ever dated, with his square jaw and thick black hair combed straight back and his gentle blue-gray eyes. He was thirty years old, three years older than she was, and he did consulting work—she wasn't sure of the details although she'd twice asked him to explain. His hours were flexible; he invariably was around to drop off and pick up May before and after her figure-skating lessons. He'd played hockey at Dartmouth, so when she explained what she was teaching May, it wasn't an altogether new language for him. A week after May's first lesson, they began dating, screwing, living (she thought) the prologue to happily-ever-after.

One of every ten vehicles coming toward them on the two-lane road is an eighteen-wheeler, a flying, ten-ton bullet. The end will be quick. The truck driver will survive, probably without a scratch. Compared with his vehicle, her Honda Civic will be little more than a tin can.

"Do you think we should call Aurora's mom?" May asks from the backseat. "What if Aurora's cell phone is broken?"

"She's fine," Lara says.

"But..." The girl's mouth trembles.

"So your dad is getting married?" Lara asks.

For a few seconds, May doesn't answer. "Uh-huh." Her voice is a quivering whisper.

"Is she nice? What does she look like?" Lara asked the same questions of Jason, and he told her, "She's nice and she's pretty. But, honestly, she's no nicer or prettier than you."

"So why are you marrying her?"

"It's a promise I made. Plans are underway." He shrugged. It was as if his decision were akin to a choice between two entrees at a restaurant.

Most women would have screamed at him, would have cursed him until he was on the floor with shame. But she nodded, as if she'd foreseen this end, as if she deserved it. "Listen," he said, "we'll continue to see each other. As friends, I mean. You're still May's coach. And, who knows, somewhere down the line, if things don't work out between me and Bethany—although I hate to start thinking like this now—and if you're still single, although, God knows, you probably won't be because you're talented and beautiful, well, maybe we'll find an occasion to be together again."

If she found what he said insulting and preposterous, she also concluded it represented an open door. All she needed was to say the right words, she thought, and she would be invited back in. When she saw him again, at the beginning of another of May's lessons, she said, "I need to see you. We need to talk."

"I'm sorry, Lara," he said. "I don't have anything else to say. If I had met you first, things might have been different." He glanced over her shoulder. She turned around to look where he was looking. May was staring at them from the doorway between the lobby and the rink. "Go warm up," Jason told her. "Coach Lara will be with you soon." A few moments passed before May turned and headed onto the ice.

"If Bethany"—Lara nearly choked on the name—"was in your life, why did you come after me the way you did? You weren't single the way you led me to believe."

"I wasn't married," he said.

"But you had a girlfriend—a fiancée."

"You're a very attractive woman, Lara. What do you want me to say? I couldn't help myself. I'm sorry. I'm very, very sorry."

"Come see me tonight," she said. "Please. One time. To say goodbye."

"I don't think—"

"Please, Jason. You owe me this." Her voice rose. He looked around the lobby. In front of the gas fireplace, Maurice Maplegate, a sixteen-year-old who'd given up hockey after sustaining two concussions and was now figure-skating three times a week, was lacing up his skates.

He had curved his body away from them, as if this would prevent him from eavesdropping.

"Okay," Jason whispered. "I'll come by tonight."

"When?"

"When I can find a moment, when I can...Let's say around nine. Maybe ten." He smiled. "All right? We'll have a cup of the strawberry tea you like. We'll talk." He smiled again. "All right?"

She nodded and found her way to the ice.

She turns the wheel to the left, kissing the center line. She does it again. Again. The fourth time, a truck coming from the other side blares its horn, and she swerves back into her space.

"What's happening?" May asks from the back seat. Lara detects the unease in her voice.

"Nothing," Lara says. "Lazy driving."

A few moments pass. "Do you think Aurora is okay?"

As if to second May's concern, Lara's cell phone rings in the seat next to hers. She checks the phone number. It's Lara's mother or father; like a quaint couple from the party-line era, they share a cell phone. She shouldn't have left her phone on, but she didn't want to miss Jason's call. He didn't say he was going to call, but what if he did? What if he called to say he'd made a mistake, he wanted her back, he—.

He doesn't have much time to make amends. She kisses the center line again, swerves back.

"What's happening?" May asks, her voice tentative, terrified.

When Jason came to her apartment, she met him at the door in a bathrobe with nothing on beneath. Her hair was slicked back, and she smelled of the lavender soap he liked to use when they bathed together. She moved aside to allow him in, but he remained in the hallway, his right hand on the wall, his left tapping his thigh. "I think it's best that we just agree to be friends," Jason told her. "I know it will be hard—for me especially. But it will make it less confusing."

"Come inside and have some tea," she said. When she saw he wasn't inclined to do so, she added, "Like you promised you would."

Her one indulgence in life was Cleopatra Strawberry Tea, imported from Egypt. Drinking the savory red tea, like hot liquid ambrosia, she could believe she had moved on from her lousy childhood, her terrible adolescence, her shitty young adulthood. She'd told Jason about all of it—the time when she was twelve and her father's best friend, during a party, stumbled drunk into her bedroom and shoved his penis in her mouth, an assault she'd been too ashamed to reveal to anyone; the pictures her high-school boyfriend snapped of her one night when they'd been stoned and naked, photographs in which she grinned at once theatrically and uncomfortably, photographs that appeared on computer screens all over town when she broke up with him; the Eastern Great Lakes Regional Figure Skating Championship, the year after she'd graduated from high school, during which, despite spending the previous nine months doing nothing but skating, burning through money she'd set aside for college, she'd fallen three times in her long program and came in fifth, one place from moving on to sectionals and a chance at the Olympics. The next few years had been a blur—three colleges, drugs she'd barely known the names of before she smoked them, swallowed them, shot them into her veins. This was followed by rehab and a relapse and, at last, a little sanity: At age twenty-seven, she was a coach for the Sherman Figure Skating Club and a part-time student at Ohio Eastern University. She was hoping to become a nurse.

After she told Jason all this, she worried he wouldn't want to see her anymore, would think she was tainted, ruined. But he had listened without judgment. "I love you even more now," he said. She felt forgiven and blessed, and after she filled his face with kisses, they made love gently, slowly, in her double bed. Afterwards, it was he who cried, as if remembering his own trauma. With him in her arms, and she in his, she felt intense happiness, as if all the doubt and self-hatred inside her had been emptied, like water drained from a tub. After he fell asleep—May was spending the night at her mother's house—darkness intruded again on her thoughts. She tried to banish it by listening to his breathing, to absorb the sweetness and sureness of it, but she feared the joy they felt would be evanescent. She wondered if it would be better to kill him—and then herself—right then, while they were flush with happiness. She even contemplated how she might do it, what weapons she had on hand. She wondered whether she could kill him so quickly he wouldn't feel pain, but would go directly from the bliss of the moment to the bliss of death. Eventually sleep dulled her fantasies.

As he stood in her hallway, she loosened the belt around her bathrobe, her right breast half exposed. "Please," she said. "I understand. I do. But I deserve one more night with you."

He resisted. Even after she'd exposed both of her breasts—breasts he had praised in the slow ecstasy of their lovemaking—he said, "I need to go. I'm sorry."

"Kiss me goodbye," she said.

This, he did.

By design, she pulled away first. She was pleased to see he was surprised. But he didn't come after more. He turned to go.

"I'm still May's skating coach, aren't I?" she asked in a voice she hoped was cool. "You won't let her leave me."

He turned back to her and smiled reassuringly. "Of course not. She loves you! We'll all be good friends."

They are twenty-eight miles from Akron. Only twenty miles of Route 45, with its north-south lanes and its 55 miles-per-hour speed limit, remain. Closer to the IcePalace, traffic will slow, congest. When would she do it, when would she have the nerve to declare, "This is the truck," and veer into the opposite lane? Between deciding and acting, perhaps a second would pass. In this second, it would be too late to save them. Would the second find her filled with regret or relieved to be a blink from the end?

A truck, as ferocious as any, approaches, its driver bearded, oblivious to her intentions. Now? Now? She hesitates. Too late. The truck rushes past, her Civic shuddering at the closeness.

"My stomach hurts," May says. "Could we stop, Coach Lara? Please, could we stop?"

May, little sweet May, would have her daddy forever, no matter whom he screwed or screwed over. Jason had married Cassie, May's mother, when he was young, a couple of years out of college, and May had come soon thereafter—an "oops," as he put it—and he never had the chance to experiment, he said.

"With drugs?" Lara asked him. "Believe me, it isn't worth it."

"No," he said, "with sex. You've heard of the Michelin Man? I'm the Missionary Man. If it isn't horizontal, it isn't happening." So she'd let him have her any way he'd wanted, even when it was uncomfortable, even when it outright hurt. She'd even—and this scared her before it happened, and shamed her now—agreed to a threesome, with the only woman she could ask, her friend from rehab who called her once a week simply to check in. This was a month after she'd told him everything about her past. Her friend—Lara can't even bring herself to conjure her name, she misses her, she knows what happened is irrevocable—asked her a dozen times if this is what she wanted. Each time she explained about Jason wanting to exhaust his fantasies before he settled down (with her, Lara, of course—or so she thought—although, it's true, he never specified) and she said, "I'll blow him, but that's it." This was okay with Jason. Perhaps it wasn't his fantasy, but it was okay.

So they all went to her place one night, drank a bottle of red wine—perhaps worried about his ability to perform, Jason didn't drink much of it—and stepped into her bedroom, where Jason stripped her as her best friend stripped down to her underwear. Soon, her friend was kneeling before him and Jason was kissing her, Lara, while also running his hands through her friend's curly red hair. She wishes she had stopped everything. No, she wishes she hadn't started anything. Before long, mercifully, it was over, and her friend didn't stay more than a minute. (Lara spoke to her on only one occasion afterwards. Her friend said, "I'll need a little time here. Bad aftertaste, you know?" It has been three months of silence.) In the immediate aftermath, after her friend left, Lara cried, and Jason said, as they lay on her bed, separated an arm's length, "There. It's over. Okay? It's over."

The only woman—girl still, although she is growing fast—who will forgive his every indiscretion and abomination is May. Little sweet May. May, whom he sometimes carries from the parking lot onto the ice when she is late for her lesson and has had to lace up her skates in his car. At these moments, he seems like a good and loving father. But sometimes he comes late to pick her up from the rink, leaving her to spend two, three, four dollars' worth of quarters on the Race Wild video game in the corner of the lobby, furiously turning the steering wheel left, right, left, right, until her virtual car spins off course and crashes into trees, farm animals, and oncoming trucks as huge and ferocious as monsters.

Let him lose what he doesn't deserve to keep, she thinks. He wants his daughter by his side because she is a different comfort than the women he fools and fucks. Let him live without anyone to forgive him. Besides, she is doing May a favor, sparing her from what will come, the humiliation and disgrace of loving men like her father.

In the backseat, May coughs, a prelude to tears, which come silently, quick strikes down her cheeks. "Please," she says softly. "Please."

"Shush," Lara says. "It won't be long now."

Another 18-wheeler approaches her from the opposite lane, its tractor unit red and angry. Now, she thinks. Now. She grips the wheel, prepares to jerk it to the left. But on the truck's window there is a glint of sunlight, like a yellow diamond, and she remembers the last time she saw May's mother. May had been practicing a backwards crossover when her feet tangled and she fell, smacking her butt and back against the ice. Lara skated over to comfort her, but the girl's crying was a hurricane. Flustered, she turned to where May's mother was, or had been, sitting in the bleachers.

Her mother—Cassie, a professor of chemistry at Ohio Eastern—approached gingerly but swiftly across the ice, the rink's fluorescent lights reflecting, diamond-like, off her glasses. When Cassie had spoken to Lara, her voice had seemed disinterested, detached, as if even an interaction with her daughter's figure-skating coach was an experiment to be studied from a passionless distance. Lara couldn't see how a woman so chilly could offer much comfort to her daughter. But she kneeled on the ice next to May, and after speaking a few words to her, began to sing—softly, a near whisper. Lara didn't know the song. But within a few seconds, the girl's crying had stopped. May sat up and pressed her head against her mother's breastbone. Her mother wrapped her arms around her—singing until they both stood and May was ready to resume her lesson.

"Home," May manages, her voice contorted from the sobs she cannot manage to suppress. "I want to be home."

"With mommy or daddy?" Lara asks. She realizes May's answer will determine whether the girl lives or dies.

"With mommy. Please. With mommy."

Violently, Lara swings her car onto the right shoulder, then into the parking lot of a vegetable stand without a name. She stops suddenly, the tires gripping the gravel. All Lara sees in the bins of the single pavilion are radishes and strawberries. Behind the vegetables and fruit, a woman, ten years older than Lara, and a girl May's age, stand, staring, blinking. Lara turns to face May. "Get out," she says.

"What?" May asks.

"Get out. Get out now."

"Why? What are—."

"Out! Now!"

May opens the door, stumbles outside. Lara does the same. She hands May her cell phone. "Call your mother," she says. May looks tiny, a trembling sprite. The cell phone falls onto crushed fruit at her feet. Lara stoops, grabs the phone, sticky with juice, and stands. "Call your mother,"

Lara repeats, returning the phone to her. May looks up, her eyes shining from tears and terror.

Lara slides back into her Civic. She doesn't look in her rearview mirror as she peels onto Route 45. Presently, she hears the grinding of her tires on the road, the whoosh of cars and trucks rushing past her in the opposite lane. She hears her heart beating against the sides of her head. Her hands squeeze the wheel. She hits a long, straight stretch. In the distance, a black truck appears, approaching furious as a storm. She turns the wheel. The truck's horn fills her ears. She smells strawberries, the scent so sweet it stings.

FALLING

The relay race against a phantom team was Jake's idea. He and Isa, his thirteen-year-old daughter, would each skate twice around the rink. His daughter would skate the first and third laps, Jake the second and anchor laps. They would use Jake's green cotton hat as the baton. If they skated the four laps in under three minutes, they would beat their imaginary opponent.

Jake had taught his daughter to skate. In memory, she hadn't been out of diapers the first time he'd brought her to the Sunday public session at the Sherman Ice Arena. Crouching, he held her under her arms as, between his legs, she slithered like an eel. They came four or five Sundays before she could skate without his help. Sometimes, of course, she fell. "If you never fall," he liked to say, "you'll never fly."

After an especially hard fall, when she was six-years-old, she complained, with tears spilling from her eyes, "You *never* fall." She said this as if, invulnerable to the ice's slickness and immune to the whims of equilibrium, he wasn't capable of falling.

"When I was learning," Jake said, "I fell all the time."

This must have been true, although he couldn't remember falling. He remembered clinging to the side of the rink until, cautious as a tightrope walker, he ventured onto the ice, his arms extended for balance. He learned in slow, careful increments, never in leaps. He admired the boys and girls who were bolder than he was. When they fell, it always looked painful. But often when they rose, they were laughing.

When his daughter turned seven, she started lessons with the Sherman Ice Arena's head instructor, Alice Maravicious, whom everyone called Alice Marvelous. After a month, his daughter could do a waltz jump and a scratch spin. Over time, she could execute half flips and flips, toe loops and loops. She could do layback spins and corkscrew spins. She mastered a lutz and an axel, a Biellmann spin and a catch-foot spin.

Before every lesson, and sometimes during a lesson (as he stood in the open gate to the rink, the cold air blowing on him), he urged her: "Keep pushing yourself."

Jake's parents had never said the same to him, and he was glad they hadn't. He would have wilted under the pressure. As a boy, he'd played several sports. He'd lasted seven out of eight games in his single pewee football season. (He'd pretended to be sick in order to miss the final game.) He'd played wide receiver, running precise routes, never finding himself anywhere near a pass. As a fifth-grader, he'd played on his elementary-school basketball team. He was known for never committing a foul nor ever being fouled. In his two Little League baseball seasons, he'd played a "deep, deep left field," as he heard his father describe it to someone over the phone.

He remembered little about his time on the diamond except one game when his team was down by a run, the bases were loaded, and he was at bat. He watched one pitch after another sail by him. With the count three balls and two strikes and the pitcher in his windup, Jake closed his eyes. He heard the ball smack the catcher's glove. He opened his eyes to strike three. The best player on his team called him a pussy. Jake should at least have swung, he said—"even with your goddamn eyes closed."

Jake was studious without being a spectacular student. His best subject was music. He played the saxophone with diligence. At the end of high school, his best friend, a trombonist named Sam, spoke about the two of them moving to New Orleans, playing in clubs, and "soaking up the life." (Sam was never specific about what "the life" might be. In its broad outlines, it involved sold-out venues and easy women.) After their high-school graduation, Sam said, "Have you packed?" He was semi-serious. Jake said, "We would never survive."

Sam tried to persuade him, but Jake foresaw disaster. Sam didn't call him a pussy, but it was clear he was disappointed. In the end, Sam did go to New Orleans; Jake went to Ohio Eastern University, played saxophone in the marching band, and earned a B.A. in music education. He'd been the band director at St. Lucy's, the local Catholic school, ever since. All in all, he'd done fine.

Jake lost touch with Sam, but another high-school friend had told him recently that she'd spotted Sam in the band of a late-night TV program. "That could have been you," she said.

Perhaps it could have been, he thought. But he still believed it was more likely he would have ended up broke and longing for home, just as it was more likely that even if he had swung on that fateful Little League pitch, he would have struck out anyway.

Nevertheless, he resented the caution in himself, even if he suspected that restraint had allowed his ancient ancestors to survive. While some prehistoric men blitzed across frozen lakes to arrive at the equivalent of late-night-TV-band careers, others fell through the ice and into evolutionary oblivion. His great-great-great-great grandparents doubtless had navigated around the lakes, clinging to boulders and tree branches, before eventually arriving in better places than they'd been before.

If, with resignation, he accepted carefulness and deliberateness in himself, he discouraged it in his daughter. "Right back up!" he would exhort after one of her failed axels. "Shake it off, sunshine!" he would shout after a botched Bielmann.

It was, perhaps, unfair to expect his daughter to do what he couldn't. But her DNA was only half his; it was likely his wife's ancestors had been more adventurous. Besides, Isa didn't know what he was incapable of—she viewed him as indestructible and fearless—and, therefore, wouldn't think caution was her inheritance. On the ice, she must have fallen a thousand times.

At a competition in Cincinnati, when Isa was twelve, she won her freestyle event with first-place votes from four out of the five judges. (Jake would have liked to ask the fifth judge, with blazing sarcasm, "What competition were you watching exactly?" He'd always kept his strongest opinions to himself, however.) As his daughter stood at the top of the podium to receive her gold medal, he imagined her saying to him, "I want to be an Olympian, Dad."

Even if he was only a high-school music teacher and his wife a licensed practical nurse whose long and inconvenient hours didn't translate into a bountiful paycheck, he wouldn't have refused. He would have said, "We'll do whatever we have to do to make your dream come true."

He imagined giving up his job and moving to some snow-coated city where she would need to train. He imagined supporting her by working in a tuna cannery or on an Arctic oilrig, every hour of labor a satisfying sacrifice. He imagined his daughter about to begin her long program in a sold-out Olympic arena somewhere in China or Norway. Before striking a pose, she would gaze up at him and acknowledge him with a wave or a wink.

But she had no illusions about becoming an Olympian. She wanted to be a lawyer.

He wondered if he dreamed his dreams for his daughter in psychic revenge for what he'd failed to do in his life or whether they were simply the dreams of any father, whether he be a former Little League hero or goat.

When asleep, he frequently had dreams of flying, and although he knew this wasn't uncommon, he nevertheless wondered if they were connected to his preference for firm footing.

Although his daughter's prowess on the ice had surpassed his long ago, she continued to indulge him by accompanying him to Sunday public-skating sessions, where they skated side-by-side, she in her $599 Paramount blades, he in rental skates. Amid the crowd of novices and wall-clingers and obnoxious boys whose daring outstripped their abilities, his daughter, with her mixture of grace and casual power, was a creature from a Greek myth, a demigoddess who deigned to inhabit, if only for the pair of hours the sessions ran, this common, frozen oval. Jake, usually the oldest person on the ice, glowed simply from the pleasure of his proximity to her.

He was aware, however, of how unexciting the public-skating sessions were for Isa. Because of the crowds, the rink prohibited advanced skaters from doing even the simplest jumps and spins. Even skating backwards was frowned on.

To forestall his daughter's boredom, Jake invented games: seeing if they could glide all the way from the blue line to the end of the rink; seeing if they could skate past twenty people in black coats in under two minutes; seeing if they could skate an impromptu program to the next pop song that blared over the public address system. (Her extemporaneous performances were gorgeous and full of flourishes; his were minimalist.)

On a November Sunday when the public session was a few minutes old and the ice was fresh, he proposed the relay race. There were perhaps a dozen people on the ice, modest obstacles to their three-minute goal. Standing on the far side of the rink, Jake put his iPhone on the ledge of the boards and tapped to the stopwatch function. Isa, who had budding breasts and hair as lush and colorful as an autumnal oil painting, discarded her pink winter jacket, flinging it onto a hockey bench. She wore a T-shirt with the name of a rock band he'd never heard of. She was, as he'd noted often recently, far closer to adulthood than to diapers.

"You ready?" he asked her.

She nodded, although he wondered if the smile she gave him suggested she was humoring him. But when he said, "Go," she skated so fast he worried she might, on the still virgin ice, be unable to hold her turn. But she whipped around the far right end of the rink and hit the next turn with the same precision. When she crossed the blue line, more than midway in her lap, only twelve seconds had passed. In less time than this, she was handing him his hat.

He fumbled it, but it didn't fall to the ice. Seconds ticked off, but now he was skating, nowhere near as fast as she had but steadily enough. He imagined a flesh-and-blood opponent: the tall, hook-nosed boy with the red-and-black hockey skates who had been eyeing his daughter since they'd arrived at the rink. He hit the first turn. Now he imagined racing against the even taller boy who, as his daughter waited for him to pick her up in front of her middle school every afternoon, always hovered near her, his black leather jacket spread around him like a vampire's cape.

He had to slow down for the next turn, but when he rounded it, he slipped past a pair of teenagers holding hands and had the length of the ice before him. He imagined both of his opponents behind him, desperate to catch up. He glanced to his left and saw his daughter against the far boards. He had expected her to be looking elsewhere, her attention diverted. But she was staring at him as if he were, in fact, engaged in a consequential race.

Faster, he told himself.

He wasn't heavy, but he weighed more than he ever had. When, seeking greater speed, he pushed off his right skate, he felt his body move with the whip-like swiftness of a bell clapper. The sensation was half-liberating, half-unsettling, akin to what he'd felt on a waterslide this past summer, his 200 pounds propelling him like a torpedo he'd fired but could not control.

A sense he was racing more than phantoms overruled his caution, however. Even as he neared the penultimate turn, where he would have to slow down, he pushed harder. He felt wild, exhilarated, cut off from caution. With another push, he decided, he would be flying. *I'm doing it*, he thought. *I'm doing it!*

He felt his right foot catch as if on a miniature hand reaching up from the ice. Presently, he was in the air, like a swimmer off the starting block. He was too surprised to be scared. A moment later, he smacked the ice, belly first, and his body shot toward the end of the rink. Hitting the boards, he crumpled like a can.

His head hadn't struck anything. The only pain he felt was in his right big toe, which, he noticed now, had punched through both its sock and the plastic or whatever old, depleted material the rental skates were made of. The skin on his toe's left side had peeled back, and his toe was oozing blood.

He realized he must be feeling pain. But a stronger emotion—exhilaration, triumph—overrode it. *I did it*, he thought. *I did it!*

What exactly "it" was, he couldn't have said, but his accomplishment made him feel at first giddy, then, unexpectedly and powerfully, proud. He remembered when he was thirteen-years-old and he and his parents had gone to a rock quarry outside of town. He'd stood on top of a boulder twenty feet above the deep water. His mother, next to him, said, "Go ahead, darling. Jump." But of course he hadn't jumped. He'd walked back down the path and slipped into the water from the shore.

But today was different: *I did it! I did it!* Tears—of relief, of jubilation—sprung from his eyes.

"Are you okay, Dad?" His daughter had skated up to him. Her face was flush with concern and, as she gazed at his bloody toe, horror. He saw what she saw: Her invincible old man, toppled, wounded, defeated. He tried to reassure her: "Yes, I'm all right. In fact, I'm—."

But, misinterpreting his tears, which poured down his cheeks, she began to cry.

A RINK, A ROPE

He comes to me at night, as ghosts do. I have left my wife sleeping in our bed. In the last trimester of her pregnancy, she has been feeling languid during the day and exhausted by sundown. On this February night, a week from my wife's due date, I fall into my usual routine, grabbing a Sam Adams from the fridge and settling in front of my laptop at the kitchen table. I turn to the window, which overlooks our backyard where soon we will be putting a swing set, a slide, a sandbox. But because it is night, I can't see the yard. I can only see myself. Or so it usually is. Tonight, however, I gaze into the face of a boy. I should be startled. But I recognize the boy as if I have been dreaming of him.

At first, he appears young. Nine or ten or eleven. But when I consider his eyes, hooded and sad, he seems as old as I am.

He makes no gesture. He doesn't smile or frown. He doesn't speak. I stand up and make my way toward the back door. When I open it and look outside, I spot him disappearing into the maple trees at the end of our yard. I think about shouting after him. But I don't have a name to call. A wind picks up and shoots across my hair. It sweeps around my body, clothed only in a T-shirt and pants and slippers. I retreat inside, rubbing my hands together, shivering.

I sit back at the table and sip my beer. It tastes bitter, the way beer did when I first drank it.

Behind the maple trees in our backyard is a trail, which winds around a forest before ending at the back of the Sherman Ice Arena where I used to play hockey. I haven't put on skates in years. Proximity to the rink isn't why we bought the house. Sandy, my wife, liked the quiet street the house was on. She liked the maple trees in the backyard. She liked the forest beyond.

We lived in our house for a year before I stepped foot in the forest. It was on a Sunday morning. An hour earlier, Sandy and I had been sitting at the kitchen table. I'd put the Lifestyles section of the newspaper at her place, the Sports section at mine. I'd made French toast. I'd cut strawberries. I'd brewed coffee and was about to pour her a cup. She held up her hand. Her smile, full of joy, scared me. I think I knew what she was going to say. "I'll have to go easy on caffeine." She paused to beam again. "I'm pregnant."

I told her I was happy. I told myself I was happy. I had become good at telling myself how I felt.

As Sandy napped, I walked into the forest. I carried a rope. I'd found it in the garage. I was going to find a tree, a big tree with a big, sturdy branch, on which to hang the rope. I told myself I was going to make a tire swing in the middle of the forest. I'd had a tire swing as a child. It was tied to an oak tree in my backyard. Because the oak tree was often the only company I had, I spoke to it as a friend. I shared secrets with the oak tree.

This would be my first act as a parent-to-be: to build a tire swing for my child. I told myself I would bring the tire later. I hung the rope.

I won't tell Sandy about the ghost. She doesn't need another worry. She is thirty-nine years old, which means her pregnancy is high risk. She's been on a special diet. Diet Cokes and chocolate cupcakes have surrendered to soymilk and salmon. She limits her exercise to walking in the swimming pool at the Y. She never picks up anything larger than a box of cereal.

Sandy and I had what might be called a Midwestern version of an arranged marriage. Reserved, awkward, and—if I am to be truthful—plain, she hadn't had an abundance of boyfriends. The man she expected to marry, she discovered after three years and a hundred promises, was married already. His wife and three sons lived two hours up the road, in Cleveland. When she turned thirty-seven, she permitted her mother to set her up with the son of her hairdresser, the handsome young man with the problematic past.

Sandy saved her inquisition for our third date, coffee at the Book and Brew, grilling me like she might one of her fifth-grade students on his times tables. When a man had cut me off in traffic, she wanted to know, why did I grab a hockey stick from the bed of his pickup truck, smash in his driver's-side window, pull him from his cab, and, as he lay on the asphalt, kick him unconscious?

"I used to have a bad temper," I said. "I've worked on the problem."

I didn't tell her I'd been following the man, hoping he would provoke me. I'd seen his bumper sticker, with its pair of hockey sticks bookending its cursive "Coach." Another of his bumper stickers said: "Rule 1: The Coach is always right. Rule 2: See Rule 1."

Had I left prison, she wanted to know, with any incurable illnesses or afflictions? She actually used the phrase "incurable illnesses or afflictions." I wondered why, given her bluntness, she hadn't simply said "AIDS."

"I survived unscathed," I told her, "if you don't count the tattoo of a dagger on my left bicep." I showed it to her. "It's from a gang I joined—a gang I had to join if I didn't want my life to become three times the hell it was."

When her face showed she expected more, I said, "I never raped anyone, and no one raped me. I've had two HIV tests since prison. Negative." I smiled. "Okay?"

Her last question: Did I think I could end up in prison again?

"I don't know."

I didn't expect to see her again.

Four months later, we were married.

Sex had been a struggle from the start. She blamed her unattractiveness; I blamed hockey injuries I'd suffered long ago. Given her age and the infrequency of consummation, I thought the odds of conception were long.

After our Sunday brunch, after my walk in the forest and her nap, she told me how thrilled she was at being pregnant, but also how nervous. Nervous, but happy. Was I happy too? She looked at me hopefully. I said, "I told you I was." She didn't seem convinced. "I am," I said. "I'm happy."

She didn't want to know the sex of our child, and because she didn't want to know, I said, "All right. We'll keep it a mystery."

I prayed for a girl. But I don't believe in prayer. And a nurse, on our last visit to the doctor's office, let slip that we would be having a boy.

When, at last, I find my way to bed, Sandy stirs beside me and extends her hand. The gesture, half wakeful, half dreamlike, is sweetly routine now. Ever since she discovered she was pregnant, she has been reaching out to me in the darkness of our bedroom, her way, I suppose, of assuring herself I am still with her in our venture into parenthood. In return, I always grasp her hand. Tonight, as usual, my grip is tender and grateful, though, with my heart racing, I am tempted to hold on to her as if she were on firm footing and I'm dangling over an abyss.

The next night, the ghost returns. I've downed three beers and have opened a fourth. I am not drunk. I know I am gazing at the same spectral figure I saw last night. The ghost's face is smooth, the ghost's eyes are soft and sad, the ghost's hair is black and full and blends into the darkness. The ghost gives me a gentle wave, a wave so slow and noncommittal it might be a playful acknowledgement of his own reflection. But then the ghost's eyes—deep-set like mine—lock on my face. He motions, and I stumble to the door.

I am not drunk; perhaps I am exhausted. I pull the door open. The ghost is already deep in my backyard, heading toward the maples. I think to shout, to ask him to wait. But I am worried Sandy, never the deepest sleeper, might wake and find me in my T-shirt and underwear calling to nothing in the black night.

The ghost slips past the maple trees. If I run, perhaps I can catch him. Or perhaps I will find myself lost and half-naked in the forest. I retreat to my kitchen table where I finish my beer and wonder what is happening to my mind.

An hour later, I slide into bed beside my wife. Her hand finds mine. I feel her welcome pulse in my palm. Did I marry her because I thought she was too old to have children? (A child would solidify the picture of normalcy I craved. But with a child, how long would our lives remain normal?) Did I hope she might somehow understand me even if I had not, and could not, explain myself—and, by understanding, somehow repair everything broken inside me? Did I marry her because I hoped her love would prove I was what I most aspired to be (but feared, in the sickness of my heart, I could never be)?

When dawn arrives, I have not slept. From her place next to me, Sandy touches the stubble on my chin, my wild hair. She notes my bleary eyes. "You need your sleep, sweetheart, because after the baby comes…" She doesn't finish, but looks at me tenderly. "It's going to be okay, you know? It's a unique experience for us, but think of all the people who've had babies, most of them with no more qualifications as parents than we have."

In her eyes, there is an invitation to tell her everything I need to tell her. One day, I vow, I will. But I don't want to upset her now, add to her worries, trouble her with the past when the future is about to burst open with uncertainty. I force a smile to my face. "I know, sweetheart. I know."

I am the manager of Jay's Sporting Goods in the West Sherman Mall, where Wal-Mart used to be. When Wal-Mart departed to open a jumbo store on Sky Lake, the West Sherman Mall's death was guaranteed. For the past six months, we have been averaging twenty customers a day. Jay's might have died even if Wal-Mart had stayed. The Internet offers a wider and cheaper selection of basketballs, baseballs, volleyballs, golf clubs. Our heating and air conditioning bills are enough to bankrupt us, but Jay, the eighty-three-year-old owner, doesn't want his business to die before he does. He is pumping his life's savings back into it. It is like giving mouth-to-mouth to a corpse.

Lately, exhausted during working hours, I have been napping in one of the tents we have on display. Today I use a hunting jacket as a pillow. When I wake up two hours later, I feel no better rested. I stagger across the rest of the day, glancing at my watch to see how little time is left.

I tell myself I am counting down to a birth. I also consider I might be counting down to its opposite.

For dinner, Sandy fixes my favorite meal, pasta with her homemade tomato and garlic sauce. Well before she has finished her portion, her eyelids fall like curtains. "Would you mind cleaning up?" she asks.

I want her to stay so as to stall the ghost's coming. But I say, "Happily." I thank her for the meal. I help her to the bathroom where she changes and brushes her teeth. I kiss her goodnight. I wait until I hear her breathing smooth into sleep before leaving her side.

If the ghost returns tonight, the third night, I will be prepared. I dress for a winter evening. I wear my winter boots, my winter jacket. I wear a scarf and a hat. I sit at the kitchen table and don't drink any beer.

Time passes. I wonder if the ghost's failure to appear is a good sign, a sign everything is going to be all right. Sandy, the baby, and I— might our future be free of trouble? The boy we have will play piano instead of hockey. He will study with a white-haired grandmother who won't so much as touch his hands to correct their placement on the keys. I work up a vision of safety, but I hear echoes, as if off the walls of a room smaller than the one I am in, of young voices familiar from long ago. I hear *his* voice—deep, commanding, revolting—whisper: "I want you to skate an extra fifteen minutes after practice." I am in prison again, but it's the prison I was in long before I was arrested, tried, sentenced. I want to scream, but I can't. I never could.

I wake up. My head is on the table. My neck aches. I look up. I see myself in the window. I recognize my slender nose, my black hair, my pale, round cheeks. I recognize both the coolness and the urgency in my eyes. As Sandy once described them, "It's like you're stepping back even as you're saying, 'Come here.'" But—no—the figure I see is younger than I am, young but serious, as if he has been told what he shouldn't yet know.

The ghost raises his right hand and places it against the window. I see it as a fortuneteller might, all its lines gentle, near invisible, save the deep-cut M, as in both of my palms. The ghost motions me outside. I know without knowing how I know: Tonight will decide everything.

I am terrified, I feel sick, but I rise, open the door, and leave my house.

I follow the ghost to the maple trees at the back of our lawn. The forest, even with trees stripped of their leaves, is darker than my yard. As we enter it, I have trouble seeing so much as my breath in front of my face. I slow my pace. The ghost slows to accommodate me.

The forest path, labyrinthine and rock hard, rises and falls. We cross a wooden bridge barely wider than a tightrope. Two dozen steps beyond the bridge, we come upon an oak tree, its lowest branch supporting a noose, illuminated in moonlight. Beneath the noose, which I don't remember tying, is a chair, which I don't remember bringing.

The ghost waits, as if to allow me to decide something. I consider how quick it would be, how easy. It would spare Sandy from finding me in the basement or the garage. It would spare her from hearing the gunshot. (She doesn't know about the gun. I've had it since the week after we married. I bought it, I told myself, to protect my new bride.) But with the ghost—only a child, after all—watching, I cannot do it. I cannot scare, scar, the boy. I shake my head, and we continue walking.

Ahead of me, the ghost slips past pine trees, and we reach the back of the Sherman Ice Arena, which looks like a barn or warehouse. The front of the arena, in contrast, is decorated—or was, when I was a boy—with children's paintings of figure skaters in blazing red dresses and hockey goalies with masks like bird cages; its glass front doors are filled with taped-on flyers announcing the Sherman Figure Skating Club's upcoming performance of *Fairy Tales on Ice* and the pewee hockey team's "Fathers versus Sons" fundraising game.

When I move to walk around the building, the ghost directs me to follow him toward a black door at the back. It gives easily when I pull. I hesitate at the threshold. I feel—although it can't be possible to feel— the ghost's hand in mine. We enter the building.

I have forgotten how large the rink is. In memory—when I am tricked into remembering—and in dreams—nightmares—it is small and dark, like a cave. But even before I hit the lights, I see, in the glow of Exit signs and whatever moonlight penetrates the windows, its vastness. With the lights on, it is even more enormous. While the revelation that the rink is larger than I remembered—that it offers more air to breathe and room to move, to escape—should be comforting, it is not. The way the lights hit the ice, creating a chilling glow, the way the corners of the rink remain dark, the way the place smells—like rental skates, like refrigerator frost, like what should be buried—all of this makes me sick, makes me furious.

Where has the boy gone? But I know, and I am terrified. I scramble around the rink to locker room number two. Beside its wooden door is a plaque, proclaiming its new name: the Robert H. Flanagan Memorial Locker Room. In smaller letters are the words: *Dedicated to the memory of an inspirational and caring man who devoted thirty-three years to the coaching of youth hockey at the Sherman Ice Arena. "A stick, a puck, a pair of skates—they are the tools to make a boy great."*

On the day the locker room was dedicated, I was arrested.

For years, I fantasized how I would kill him. I fantasized about murder's prelude: strapping him to the bench in this locker room as if it were an operating table, gagging him with a hockey puck, slashing at his neck and his groin with a hockey stick. For every time he touched me— ten slashes. For every time he violated me—a wound as deep as I could make.

His death was the worst news I could have received. I couldn't kill him now. I couldn't even expose him for what he was. His reputation as a selfless, devoted, Christian builder of young men was secure.

In prison, I used to speak once a week with Father Jacob, who said the world's evils cannot be made good by vengeance. Better, he said, to forgive. Or if one cannot forgive, he said, better to put whatever wrong one has suffered out of mind—to forget—and move on. "I tried, Father," I say now outside the door of the locker room. "I tried and I succeeded. Look, Father. I have a normal life. I'm a married man, with a son on the way. I've forgotten. I've moved on."

But from behind the locker room's locked wooden door, I hear Coach Flanagan's deep voice, its false reassurances, its murmurs of affection and praise. I hear, and with the same terror as always, the grown man's desire beneath his words. He is with the boy, and I know what is going to happen next. The thought fills me with rage, and I kick and kick at the wooden door. I am conscious of a slicing pain up my right leg, but it doesn't deter me. I slam my shoulder against the door. I kick it again.

When I again hurl my shoulder against the door, it gives and I am inside the locker room. "Where are you?" I scream. "Where do you have him?" I open lockers. If they are locked, I kick them; I punch them; I shoot my knee into them. When I am done, they are car crashes. "You son of a bitch! You sick monster!" I rush into the shower room, pull soap dispensers from the walls. I fling open every bathroom stall door, expecting to find him, his pants around his knees, the boy naked and terrified and crouched over the toilet, about to barf his shame and confusion.

I hear my coach's whisper, urgent and smooth: "I love you, and this is proof of my love. You're my special boy. You're my favorite little player. But don't tell anyone because what we have is a secret, and no one will believe you anyway."

"Where the fuck are you?" I yell, spinning around. "Where are you hiding him? Goddamn you!" I slam a stall door so hard it cracks off its hinges and clatters to the floor.

I stalk out of the bathroom, then the locker room. I see them, the coach and the boy, at the far end of the ice. Coach Flanagan is showing the boy how to shoot a slapshot. I hear his words, authoritative and encouraging, instructive and warm. I find myself, against everything I know, stopping to listen. I am confused, as I once was, lulled and seduced by the voice's gentleness, its confident cadences, its kindness and authority. *You are special. You are my star.*

Is this why I never told my parents? Because despite what he did to me in the locker room after my teammates left, I liked—I needed—what he said to me on the ice?

"No!" I scream. I grab what is hanging from the wall—a fire extinguisher—and rush onto the ice. I can no longer see the coach and the boy, but I know they are concealed in the rink's shadows, so I spray everywhere. I spray the four corners of the ice. I spray the benches, the penalty boxes, the announcer's booth. When the foam has exhausted itself, I hurl the extinguisher into the scoreboard above me, smashing lights. Pieces fall like hard snowflakes.

How long has an alarm been sounding? How long have sirens been blaring? How long has my cell phone been throbbing against my thigh?

I read my wife's text: in labor where r u come home now.

I see police lights swirl in the windows at the front of the arena. I rush off the ice, listing and sliding but somehow holding my footing. I race out of the arena's back door and sprint into the forest, into darkness.

Where am I? How will I find my way home? I pinch my cell phone, its light illuminating only a foot or two of the path. My hand shakes, and my phone slips from my grasp. My foot collides with it, and the phone shoots into the underbrush. I curse but don't stop. I run and run. Presently, I trip and fall, my palms and knees and chest slamming into the rock-hard ground.

When I look up, I see the chair and the noose, which swings in a breeze. Above the noose are tree branches and cold, distant stars. "Is this what you want?" I ask. Who am I speaking to? My sick, dead coach? Myself? Or am I speaking to whoever let this happen to me—to God?

I rise, climb on the chair, and pull the rope over my neck. But I see the boy, standing pale against the trunk of the oak tree. He isn't smiling; he isn't frowning. I see no judgment in his eyes. He will understand, won't he—he will understand why I have to do this, why I need to abandon him?

But what will he understand if I don't explain?

I remove the noose from my neck, step from the chair, and stagger toward him. "You'll be better off without me," I say. "Your mother will be twice the parent I could ever be. You'll be better off without my rage and my poisoned mind."

But what does my son know of rage and poisoned minds? He is only a ghost of what is yet to be born and borne.

I fall against the oak tree, its bark like the rough, wrinkled skin of someone I loved long ago. I wrap my arms around its solid body. I am weak; I fear I will collapse. But I feel the tree return my embrace, as if offering me a stay of execution. My son, beside me, small arms spread wide and trusting against the firm bark, holds on too, imitating me.

THE RINK GIRL

Her family moved to town from Omaha on Christmas Eve. Her father and mother are the new managers of the Sherman Ice Arena, which, thanks to the coal-baron millionaire who owns it, is open all year. It is mid-January now, skating season. Half the town goes to the public skate on Saturday afternoon, the experience like walking down the aisles of a sold-out show. *Excuse me. Sorry. Hey—watch it!*

Walt waits in the long line to rent skates. Behind the counter is the Rink Girl. She isn't pretty. This is what every boy in the tenth grade says. Acne coats the sides of her face like raindrops on a window. Her brown hair looks oily, and its curls are petals of a wilted flower. Her eyes, however, are a dazzling hazel.

"Size?" she says. She looks him over. "Wait. Aren't you in the geography class before mine?" Geography, a tenth-grade elective. His parents insisted he enroll, so he wouldn't be ignorant of the world. "Walt, right?"

"Yeah."

"What size, Walt?"

He tells her, and she retrieves a pair of night-blue skates from the shelf behind her. The skates are the newest the rink owns, she says. "The gray ones have been here since 1947. The brown ones? Since the Civil War."

She looks to her left, out the windows of the double doors and onto the rink. Ten minutes after the start of the session, it's packed. Shaking her head, she turns back to him. He hears someone grumble in the line behind him: "What is this, the post office?"

"How much do you like skating?" the Rink Girl whispers, her voice as intimate as a lullaby.

"I like it fine," he says.

"Come back at midnight."

"Is there another public skate?"

"Come back at midnight," she repeats.

He wakes up as if to an alarm. The red numbers of his digital clock radiate the time: 11:42. He fell asleep convinced the Rink Girl wasn't serious about midnight. There's only one way to know for sure. He exchanges his pajamas for the clothes on his floor. His house is asleep.

Silver, his dog, acknowledges him with three thumps of his tail before closing his eyes again. He steps outside.

The rink isn't more than a mile from his house. Because the night is clear and full of stars and the roads are free of snow and ice, he rides his bike. He makes it to the rink in minutes. But the door is locked, and when he taps like a hopeful fool, no one answers. If Brian and Ben could see him now, they would laugh all week. They were supposed to join him at the rink this afternoon, but they watched football instead.

"Hey." He turns to the voice behind him. "You're early." The Rink Girl smiles. In the bright-dark night, in her gray overcoat and bowler hat, she looks like a bohemian detective. She inserts a key into the rink's front-door lock, turns it, and pushes the door in. "After you."

It is darker than night inside. Then it's as light as a party. The Rink Girl calls him over from her spot behind the counter. "Do you want the same boots?" she asks.

"Sorry?"

"The same skates. Do you want the same skates you had on today?"

"Sure," he says.

She places the night-blue skates on the counter. Her own skates are white, with red hearts on the toes. As she laces them up in the lobby, he stares at them. "It was either hearts or skulls," she says. "Next time, I'm going with skulls."

She kills the lights in the lobby and clicks them on in the rink. She pushes open the double doors and leads him to the gate. She snaps it open and draws it in. "Gentlemen first," she says. He isn't prepared for how smooth the ice is—he is used to it being gnawed by a hundred blades—and he finds his feet flying forward and his head plummeting backward.

She catches him under his shoulders. "Careful, cowboy." She rights him with surprising strength. He glides onto the immaculate ice. She moves in front of him with the ease of a bird soaring across the sky, her coat like wings.

He follows her over several laps of the rink before she slows to skate beside him. "What's your story?" she asks.

"What do you mean?"

"Who are you? What do you want to be when you grow up? What's your favorite sin?" She laughs as if she isn't serious. But then she gazes at him as if she is.

He edits his answers, so he'll sound cool, adventurous. But she follows up with more questions, and he ends up telling her the truth: His name is Walt Taylor. He is fifteen years old. His best sport is swimming. His favorite class is geography. (He wouldn't have said this before today, but he is convinced of it now.) He doesn't have a girlfriend. He last kissed a girl when he was in the sixth grade. When he was younger, he sometimes practiced kissing on his dog. He doesn't know what his favorite sin is because he feels guilty even when he doesn't sin. He wants to be in the movies. He'd settle for being a newscaster in Cleveland.

"All right," he says, "now you."

Her name is the Rink Girl. No, of course it isn't. But she knows people call her the Rink Girl. She doesn't mind. She loves skating rinks. She loves how they smell. She loves how the Zamboni mows them clean, leaving tiny, shimmering puddles. Her parents, who won a bronze medal in pairs skating at the World Championships a hundred years ago, moved to the United States from Russia when they were in their early twenties in order to join the Skating Sensations tour. This lasted two and a-half years. They have been the managers of six rinks, the last outside of Omaha.

"What happened in Omaha?" he asks.

"The city couldn't afford to operate the rink anymore. It's a ghost building now."

"That won't happen here."

She shrugs. "Let's hope."

They skate a loop around the rink in silence. "Are you bored yet?" she asks.

"What?" he says.

"Boys tend to get bored with ice skating."

"So you've skated with a lot of boys."

"My brother," she says. "If he doesn't have a stick, a puck, and a net, he doesn't want to be anywhere near a rink."

"What grade is he in?"

"He's in the Army."

"In the war?"

She nods. She is silent as she skates.

"I'm not bored," he says.

She says, "You know what my favorite sin is? Disobedience."

"Oh," he says. "So your parents don't know you're here?" He looks around as if they might be hiding in the shadows.

"They do," she says. "But they don't know *you're* here." She smiles and dashes in front of him. "Catch me," she says.

It's impossible. After they have done a dozen laps, she calls across the rink: "You don't have to go the same direction I'm going." In a louder voice, she says, "Catch me any way you can."

But she is too skilled and swift for him. He fails even to touch her. Cramping from exhaustion, he leaves the ice. She joins him in the second row of the three-tiered bleachers. Panting, he says, "Trying to...catch you...is like...trying to...catch light."

She touches his knee. He looks at her hand, then at her face. Her dazzling hazel eyes. Her pimples like small pink jewels. Her lips.

Her hand meets his. He squeezes it, and she squeezes back.

"This doesn't mean I'm going to kiss you," she says.

She says they ought to leave. "I could probably teach you to be the world's greatest figure skater in the next couple of hours," she says. "But then neither of us would have a reason to come back. You would be on a Wheaties box, and I would be the Annie Sullivan of skating teachers."

"Who's Annie Sullivan?" he asks.

"She coached Helen Keller to gold at the '24 Olympics."

Outside, the sky is as luminous as he's ever seen it. She walks up steps to the street and is about to cross. "What about a kiss?" he asks, surprised by his boldness.

She turns around. "Maybe when you catch me," she says. There is a pause. "Hell, that will never happen." She skips down the stairs and plants an ice-cool kiss on his lips. The sensation is like winter's first snowfall. "Goodnight."

On Monday morning in the third-floor hallway at Sherman High School, she doesn't acknowledge his wave. At the door to the geography classroom at the fifth-period bell, he touches her shoulder. She looks at him as if he's a spider's web with which she tangled on a walk in the woods.

At the end of the school day, he walks home, disconsolate. As soon as he steps into the alley off Lye Street, she leaps from behind a green garbage can. He is too happy to be startled. But remembering how she treated him today, he narrows his eyes. "What's up?" he says.

"I know I ignored you at school," she says. "But I did it for your own good."

"What do you mean?"

"If your friends knew you liked the Rink Girl, you wouldn't hear the end of their teasing."

"I can handle them," he says, although without confidence.

"Besides, it's easier this way," she says. "We can concentrate on school when we're at school."

"And after school, we can do what we want."

"No, we have to do our homework."

"Are you serious?" The disappointment in his voice is as evident as a tuba in an orchestra of piccolos.

Softly, she says, "My parents don't want me to grow up to be the Rink Woman. And they don't want me to join the Army like my brother. They're thinking doctor, lawyer, CEO of the world. So they want me to spend every afternoon and evening between Sunday and Friday in the company of books, calculators, and computers."

"I see," Walt says.

"So Saturday night is all we have." She pauses. "Saturday night and now."

She pulls him toward her. Squatting behind the green garbage can, they touch each other's ears and tangle tongues.

At the rink on Saturday night, she dazzles him with what she can do.

"What was that?" he asks. "A double axel?"

"Is that an official jump?" she says.

"I think so."

"I never had a lesson in my life—my parents were always too busy to teach me—so I don't know any of the real jumps or spins or moves. I've made up my own. I'll teach them all to you. This one I call the Floating Phantom."

She dives into the air, her body—he swears—horizontal to the ice before she rolls over as if on an invisible bed and, with her arms in front of her like a sleepwalker, returns to the cold surface.

"This one I call the Sit Up." She jumps into the air, kicks both legs straight in front of her, and curls up to touch her toes before sticking her legs back on the ice.

"And this I just call Crazy." She leaps into the air, summersaults, and lands without falling, without even trembling.

"Wow," he says. "Wow."

"Which one do you want to learn first?"

He considers. "How about we begin with you teaching me how to skate backwards?"

She taps her lips. "Boring," she says. "But all right." She steps in front of him, facing him. "Put your hands up like you're touching a wall."

When he does, she puts her hands in his. Neither of them is wearing gloves. But if his hands were cold, they are no longer. For years when he sees a couple standing like this, facing each other, palms pressed together, fingers interlocked, he will remember her, and he will feel sweetly disoriented as if he had time-traveled.

Gently, she pushes into him, instructing him how to move his skates like he's using them to draw ovals in the ice.

After several minutes, she says, "I think you have it," and she gives him a push and he glides backward, as if on air, to the end of the rink.

The Rink Girl does not insist he practice his skating, but if he is to become as good as she is, or even half as good as she is—if he is to impress her at all—he must practice. So he comes to the public sessions on Wednesday and Thursday nights, fighting past mad-dashing eight-year-olds in hockey masks and trios of linked-armed twelve-year-old girls and divorced men and women on first dates as awkward as their skating.

On occasion, he glimpses the Rink Girl at a desk in the small office behind the rental skates, a textbook spread in front of her, a pen or pencil in her hand. Always, he lingers, wanting her to see him and beam, wanting to leap over the counter, slide up beside her, whisper into her brown hair.

During a school assembly in mid-March, he finds himself, by luck of the way homeroom classes occupy the rows of seats in the auditorium, sitting beside her. Police officers occupy the stage, railing against drugs or graffiti or something else subversive. She won't look at him, won't acknowledge him with anything even so small as a smile. He is terrified of making such a move himself, worried she will respond in a manner as cold as the ice on which she thrills him.

"Say no to temptation," he hears a police officer say. "Say no to impulsiveness, to wildness, to irrational behavior. Say no, no, no."

He feels his hand fill, remarkably, with hers. She leans over to him, kisses his ear, whispers, "Say yes, yes, yes."

As a skater, he isn't improving as quickly as he wants. He skates backward now, but he is far from mastering even the move she calls the

Semi-Sane, which is a leap, a landing on two feet, and a spin into a backward skate. "Watch," she says. When she does it, it seems as simple as playing hopscotch. But when he tries to imitate her, he falls.

"Again," she says.

He falls.

"Again."

He falls.

"Again."

He falls. He falls. He falls. He falls. He falls. He falls.

He succeeds.

"Again."

He falls.

"Again."

He is in love, but no one knows it. He confides in no one. Not his parents. Not his older brother. Not Brian and Ben. To tell, he thinks, might be to awaken him from his dream or to have it trivialized with "Isn't that sweet" or with teasing or with (in Ben's and Brian's case) rude remarks about her pimples or her oily hair or the way she smells of old skates.

"Again."

He falls.

"Again."

He falls.

"Again."

He falls.

"I'll show you something special if you do it right."

He succeeds.

In the center of the ice, she lifts her blue sweater slowly. Thinking she is going to show him her breasts, his heart chugs like a manic choo-choo train. But she stops short, the bottom of the sweater a barricade. Now he sees her revelation: a red scar beginning at her navel and shooting like an angry bolt toward her breastbone.

"What happened?" he asks.

"I was doing a combination of the Buddha and the Ballerina. My blades had just been sharpened. They might as well have been ninja knives."

"It's amazing."

"You were probably hoping I'd show you my tits."

"I mean, it's amazing that you made a mistake. I've never seen you—."

"Who said anything about making a mistake? I tried to do a mash up of two irreconcilable moves. It's like dancing over the canyon of a paradox."

"Excuse me?"

"You did want to see my tits, didn't you?"

God yes, he thinks.

"Well, it's your lucky night."

In the beginning of June, he turns sixteen. This is good fortune. He needs an automobile because his summer job, to which he applied nine months earlier, is at a YMCA overnight camp in Bellefontaine, Ohio, four hours from Sherman. The automobile wasn't originally a necessity. He'd planned to spend his entire summer on the campgrounds. But if he wants to see the Rink Girl, which is akin to asking if he wants to live, he'll need to drive back from Bellefontaine every Saturday.

Each employee of Camp Belle is allowed one night off a week. Naturally, everyone wants Saturday night. Seniority dictates who is assigned what day, however. As a junior counselor, Walt sees he will be stuck with Tuesdays and Thursdays. On his first day at camp, he thinks about quitting. But his parents—his accursed parents—have opted to trade houses over the summer with a couple from Vallebona, Italy. He has nowhere to stay in Sherman.

In exchange for their Saturday nights, he surrenders to his fellow counselors his baseball glove, his fishing rod, his iPod. He doesn't miss any of it, except, perhaps, his baseball glove when, playing leftfield during the camper-counselor softball game, he catches a fly ball with his bare palm.

Because he is permitted to leave camp after dinner on Saturday, he has no problem arriving at the rink by midnight. The return trip's timeline proves tighter. He leaves the rink as the sun slips its first light over the horizon like a lover sliding a letter under a door. He crushes the gas pedal to make it back by Sunday breakfast, which, fortunately, begins only at nine-thirty.

Over the succeeding days, he catnaps when he can in order to recuperate the sleep he lost in staying up all night. By the time Saturday comes again, he is fully rested. He doesn't tell the Rink Girl about the lengths he goes to see her. He doesn't want her to think he's as lovesick as he is.

The Rink Girl spends her summer weekdays at a series of science and math camps in Cleveland and Columbus. Sometimes he hears her mumbling what sound like formulas or Latin mottos. *Supra glaciem stemus, cum corde ignis.*

She teaches him the Slam, which is a series of short jumps followed by a high jump. She teaches him the Slow Mirror, in which one side of his body repeats the movements of the other. She teaches him the Backward Peek-a-Boo, in which he skates backward and pokes his head between his legs to see where he's going.

Despite the scoreboard above the east end of the rink with its red-numbered clock, dawn always surprises them. At first light, they kiss with the fury of hummingbirds stealing dew from the flowers of a butterfly bush.

On the Saturday night before the beginning of school, when he is back from camp, she isn't at the rink. In her place is a note with his name: *Had to leave town. Left the door open. The ice is yours.*

But without her, the ice feels—and he realizes how odd it is to think this way—cold. The rink feels cavernous and lonely, like a ship abandoned at sea. He drifts around the ice like a shipwrecked sailor hoping to find an island. He leaves after less than an hour, then stays up all night, wondering where she is and what might be wrong.

On the first day of school, he stands beside the main entrance to Sherman High like a soldier. He doesn't care if she doesn't speak to him. He only wants to see her. For the past twenty-four hours, he has done nothing but worry—irrationally, he knows—that she is gone forever, off to bless another rink in another town, to turn another boy's Saturday nights into magic. The last bell rings, and he slinks inside the building and slouches to his homeroom.

But at the change of classes before third period, he sees her at the end of the hall. He is so relieved he fails to realize they are approaching each other with the speed of speed skaters. They collide, and she is sobbing a hurricane. "What's wrong?"

"My brother," she says.

"What happened? He didn't…Is he…?"

He feels her nod against his shoulder. Her tears are ferocious.

There is an audience around them. But the bell rings, and the hallway empties.

"We had to meet the body," she says. "We buried him in the National Cemetery, in Virginia."

"I'm sorry," he says. After a moment, he adds, "I wish I had more to say."

"There isn't more to say."

At school, it is impossible to pretend they aren't boyfriend and girlfriend. But perhaps owing to her brother's death, news of which everyone seems to have heard, they are left alone. They eat their lunches at the far end of the football field, in a corner where the grass is softest. They walk home together every day. In the wake of her brother's death, there is a solemnity to their conversations. Even their Saturday nights on the ice assume a mournful aura, the jumps, spins, and moves she teaches him bearing such names as "Cerement" ("a shroud," she explains helpfully), "Heaven's Door," and, defiantly, "Death Be Not Proud."

One Saturday night, she gives him a pair of ice skates, black with red eyelets. She doesn't say to whom they belonged, but he knows. They fit perfectly.

"I think it's time," she says at the beginning of October.

"Time?"

"To do a duet."

His role is simple. He skates forward, from one end of the rink to the other. She moves around him like water moves around rocks in a rippling stream. "Now backward," she says. He skates backward, and she flies around him, a predator about to devour him. No, only a butterfly looking to land.

Which she does, in his arms. "I feel better," she says.

In the middle of October, she invites him to have dinner at her house. From outside, her house looks ordinary: faded brick, ornamental wooden shutters with chipping white paint, a covered front porch with a pair of rocking chairs. Inside, he discovers a long hallway whose walls, top to bottom, are lined with photographs of her brother. "My parents say if the photos went halfway around the world," the Rink Girl whispers, "it would be too short a distance by half."

Presently, her parents come to meet him. Her father is tall and burly, with a beard that could hide a small child. Her mother is short and thin, with dyed orange hair in the style of a broom end. "I see you've met our son," she says. Walt looks around, as if there might be someone else in the room. But of course there is: The walls are alive.

"I'm sorry for your loss," he says.

But they appear not to have heard him. "Handsome, isn't he?" her mother says.

Her father adds, "And smart as a scientist."

Her parents have already eaten—or perhaps they aren't hungry—because after a minute more of polite talk, they excuse themselves and disappear. The Rink Girl waves him deeper into the house, into the kitchen, where she pulls pots and pans from cabinets. "What would you like to eat?" she asks. "Name anything."

"Anything?"

"Anything."

You, he wants to say.

"I don't know. Well." *Right now I'd like to taste the right corner of your mouth*. His mother is an excellent cook: "Sea bass with rice pilaf, carrots au gratin, and a Caesar salad."

"Excellent," she says. "Next time, I'll know. Tonight we'll have peanut butter and jelly sandwiches. Any objections?"

He has none.

As they eat their sandwiches with a side of apple sauce in lunch-sized containers, he says, "Where did your parents go?"

She shrugs. "They haven't been here in anything more than body since my brother died. If I were a different kind of daughter, I would take advantage of the situation by, I don't know, hauling you upstairs and losing my virginity to you under the poster of Amelia Earhart on my ceiling."

"You have a poster of Amelia Earhart on your ceiling?"

She looks at him askance. "That's what you found most interesting about what I just said?"

On the ice, he learns, or half learns, or watches her demonstrate, the Rabbit, the Monkey, the Horse, and the other nine signs of the Chinese zodiac.

"Someday," she says, "I'll teach you the Big O."

"What's the Big O?"

She only smiles.

Several times she tries to sneak him into her house—"to introduce you to Amelia Earhart," in her winking words—when she thinks her parents aren't home, but one or both is always present. One time, her parents are entertaining the Medev family from Moscow. If the Rink Girl's father was ursine, Lev Medev—tall, bearded, and with a girth so large he might have eaten a bear—is doubly so. He is the owner of the Moscow Circus on Ice, which is in town to do a one-night show in Sherman. The Medevs have a son, whom the Rink Girl's parents have been encouraging her to spend time with.

"I hope he's twice as ugly as his old man," Walt tells her, feeling jealousy burn so hot in him he could cook a four-course meal on his chest.

"I thought he would be" is all the Rink Girl says in reply.

She likes him. Damn it all. Could she like him more than she likes me? Please, God, no. Now Walt's chest blazes like the center of the sun.

The next Saturday night, the Rink Girl brings a pair of blankets onto the ice. "Don't pretend you don't know what these are for," she says.

"Oh," he says.

"Close," she says. "The Big O." She laughs and pulls him down toward the unforgettable.

"This is it," he says afterwards—or after the third afterwards. "This is the summit of my existence on earth."

"Time to move to Mars," she says, kissing him again.

But it is she who might be moving. The Medevs have asked her parents to manage their five rinks in Moscow as well as the amusement park next door to a prison that briefly housed Alexandr Solzhenitsyn. "There's a ride called One Minute in the Life of Ivan Denisovich," she says. She looks him over. "You don't think I'm funny?"

"I know you're funny," says Walt. "But I don't know who Ivan Denisovich is. And I can't stand the thought of you moving to Moscow."

"My parents haven't been happy since Leo died," she says. "They might see this as a chance to start over—to be reborn where they were born."

They live as if she might leave tomorrow. Saturday nights at the rink become every night at the rink. Some mornings, Walt doesn't know how he manages to rise from his bed. He is deliciously, deliriously exhausted. The holidays come. Halloween. Thanksgiving, Christmas. At midnight on each, he is at the rink.

On New Year's Eve, she tells him her parents have decided they won't be moving to Moscow after all. They celebrate by skating the New Year's Toast, the New Year's Resolution, and Auld Lang Syne. The latter is the easiest. They stand next to each other, wrap their arms around each other's shoulders, and sway.

The next night when Walt arrives at the rink, he sees a pair of two-by-fours nailed across the front entrance. Something awful must have happened inside, he thinks. A gas leak. A burst pipe. A hockey player gone berserk with his stick. But the Rink Girl, behind him now, says, "The rink is closed. The owner is tearing it down to build condos."

Walt turns to her. Her tone tells him she is serious. But he cannot refrain from asking, as if out of an obligation to hope, "Are you joking?"

"The owner told my parents the rink is too expensive to maintain," she says. "He blames it on global warming and sixty-degree winter days."

"But he's creating global warming with his coal. If he would shut down his coal mines, he could keep his rink." The world suddenly seems sinister and doomed. "What happens now?"

She shakes her head. "Moscow," she says. "We leave in three days."

Global warming has taken the evening off. Walt's breath pours out of him as thick as smoke from a coal-fired power plant. What world will he be living in when the Rink Girl is gone? "What? You can't be serious. Are you serious?"

"I would love to be joking."

"You don't have to move," he says. "You can stay here. You can finish high school in Sherman. I'll talk to my parents. You can live with us."

She smiles softly, and he knows it's a prelude to words he doesn't want to hear. "I thought of this," she says. "I thought of a hundred solutions." Her breath fills the air between them. "My parents would miss me too much. Because of what happened to my brother, they want me close."

They walk around the rink, checking windows, checking doors. But nothing gives, nothing opens. They come to the last door, on the edge of the forest at the back of the rink. He kicks it with his black winter boots. He punches it with his bare hands. Bang. Bang. Bang. He finds a brick behind him and smashes it against the wood. Bang. Bang. Bang. He tries his boots again, the brick again. Bang. Bang. Bang. Bang-bang-bang. He drops to his knees.

"I guess no one's home," she says.

He turns. She is at the edge of the woods. A step backwards, and she would be swallowed whole by the oak and maple trees. "Fate isn't our friend," she says with a resignation he has never heard from her. "But who marries her high-school sweetheart nowadays, anyway?"

"Half the people in this town," he says, sweeping his hands over the dark wood.

"How happy are they?"

"A thousand times happier than I'll be when you're gone."

On their last night together, the Rink Girl proposes they go with their skates to Murderer's Cove on Sky Lake, where the ice is frozen solid. In the twenties and thirties, Murder's Cove hosted criminal activity ranging from bootlegging to assassination. Or so local legend goes. Now it's a refuge for teenage lovers who lack a private place to crawl into each other's bodies.

The sky is full of stars, as if from Acamar to Zubeneschamali, they had thrown back the curtain of night to spy on love's last ice dance. He watches the Rink Girl skate across the cove. When she is at the far end, barely visible against a background of pine trees, he skates toward her with a rage he wouldn't have imagined himself capable of. She is facing the trees, her back to him, when he slices to a stop behind her. "Why aren't you furious at the world?" His voice is half accusatory, half perplexed. "Why aren't you as sad as I am?"

But when she turns to him, he sees she is crying, and not gently. "Oh," he says, embarrassed and strangely relieved. They fall into each other. He slides his arms into her coat and around her waist. He pulls her toward him.

"What are we going to do?" she asks.

"Run away with me," he says.

"I wish I could."

"What would it take to convince you?" he asks. "I'll do anything. I'll walk home on my skates. I'll sing all night to the stars." He pauses. "Wait," he says. "I know. I'll show you I can do the most difficult jump you ever tried to teach me." He pushes back from her, onto the starlit cove. "No, I'll do an even harder jump. I'll do the jump you only spoke to me about. What did you call it? The End of the World, right?"

"It's impossible to do an End of the World," she says. "Even I can't do it. You haven't even done a Mini Apocalypse."

"You'll see," he says. "If you say you'll run away with me, I'll do it." The energy of superheroes flows in his veins; he feels he could leap and grab hold of a star. He isn't going to lose her. He's going to do the impossible and they are going to live together forever, their lives always sweet, always delicious.

"If I do it, will you run away with me?"

She nods, a nearly invisible gesture.

"Promise?"

This time there is conviction: "I promise."

"All right," he says. He skates up to her, cups her cheeks, kisses her. "Here goes."

He skates to the center of the cove, fifty yards from her, before halting and swirling around. She is gray against a black background, but she is all the color of his life. He skates toward her with a power he has never possessed. His skates feel like they are barely touching the ice. He moves fast, faster. Ten feet from her, he soars, streaking toward the stars. He does a complete twist and a half, and he is still climbing, like a roaring rocket. He dips his head toward the ice and curls his skates toward the sky. Presently, his skates fall and his head rises, a delirious somersault—and another! Now he is coming down clean. He anticipates her joy, and his, and how their happiness will see them past hardship and doubt, will outblaze the stars.

His skates strike the ice straight and perfect. He lifts his arms in triumph, but at the same time he feels the ice give and open around him. He plummets like a stone.

Years pass, and every breath without her is like ice water in his lungs.

ACKNOWLEDGMENTS

I am grateful to the editors of the magazines and journals in which these stories first appeared.

Windmill: "Dear Kristi Yamaguchi"
Michigan Quarterly Review: "The Sleeping Beauty"
Notre Dame Review: "Fifty," "The Drive"
St. Ann's Review: "Duets"
Lake Effect: "The Skater and the Soldier"
THAT Literary Review: "Profiles in Paranoia"
Cleaver: "Tornado"
Raleigh Review: "Goodbye, Goodbyes"
The MacGuffin: "Falling"
Juxtaprose: "A Rink, a Rope"
Ploughshares: "The Rink Girl"

ABOUT THE AUTHOR

Mark Brazaitis is the author of eight books, including *The River of Lost Voices: Stories from Guatemala*, winner of the 1998 Iowa Short Fiction Award; *The Incurables: Stories*, winner of the 2012 Richard Sullivan Prize and the 2013 Devil's Kitchen Reading Award in Prose; and *Truth Poker: Stories*, which won the 2014 Autumn House Press Fiction Competition. He also wrote the script for the award-winning Peace Corps film *How Far Are You Willing to Go to Make a Difference?*